THE SILENT KNIGHT

L. B. Martin

Copyright © 2023 L. B. Martin

All rights reserved

The characters and events portrayed in this book are fictitious. Any similarity to real persons, living or dead, is coincidental and not intended by the author.

No part of this book may be reproduced, or stored in a retrieval system, or transmitted in any form or by any means, electronic, mechanical, photocopying, recording, or otherwise, without express written permission of the publisher.

ISBN: 9798867741631 (paper)

This book was edited by Terry Hooker, Blue Dahlia Publishing House, LLC

Cover design by: Samuel Greenwald
Library of Congress Control Number: 2018675309
Printed in the United States of America

Dedication

For all those who fall down but get back up again. I see you. I am you.

And for those that want to get railed by a big military man, this is my Christmas gift to you.

"Christmas will always be as long as we stand heart to heart and hand in hand."

-DR. SEUSS

CONTENTS

Title Page
Copyright
Dedication
Epigraph
Playlist
Prologue
Chapter 1 — 1
Chapter 2 — 6
Chapter 3 — 14
Chapter 4 — 19
Chapter 5 — 25
Chapter 6 — 32
Chapter 7 — 40
Chapter 8 — 47
Chapter 9 — 52
Chapter 10 — 60
Chapter 11 — 66
Chapter 12 — 70
Chapter 13 — 81

Chapter 14	88
Chapter 15	96
Chapter 16	105
Chapter 17	111
About The Author	117
Books In This Series	119
To learn more about l. b. martin	123

PLAYLIST

Inside Her Head – Bryce Savage

It's Beginning To Look A Lot Like Christmas – Michael Bublé

Safe Haven – Ruth B.

Baby It's Cold Outside – She & Him

Adore You – Harry Styles

Carry You (feat. Fleurie) - Ruelle

All I Want For Christmas Is You – Mariah Carey

Fire On Fire – Sam Smith

Heal – Tom Odell

Have Yourself A Merry Little Christmas – Sam Smith

Christmas Tree Farm – Taylor Swift

Curiosity – Bryce Savage

Twin Flame – Machine Gun Kelly

Silent Night – Lauren Daigle

Bad Things – Machine Gun Kelly & Camila Cabello

Rise Up – Andra Day

Cozy Little Christmas – Katy Perry

Like It's Christmas – Jonas Brothers

Santa Tell Me – Arianna Grande

Wonder – Shawn Mendes

Holly Jolly Christmas – Michael Bublé
With You This Christmas – Why Don't We
Spotify

PROLOGUE

5 days til Christmas...

Sarah

Cold air blasts me in the face as I step out of the studio doors. Immediately, I regret not grabbing my jacket before I left. I stepped out for just a moment, but the winter air is already seeping into my bones, making goosebumps erupt over my skin. I head to the car, seeing only one other person on the other side of the parking lot. He's a long way off so I pick up my pace and hurry. I need to grab the large donation box full of presents for the Toys For Tots charity. I didn't bring them in earlier, an action I'm regretting now. A cool wind whips my hair into my face and a tremor wracks through my body. Finally arriving at my car, I unlock the trunk and pull the large box closer. An eerie feeling passes over me, giving me chills. I settle the box back into the trunk and look up at the parking lot, seeing the man from earlier has moved closer to me. Hurriedly, I pull the box of presents from the car before I can close the trunk I feel his presence behind me like a predator stalking its prey.

"That's a nice car ya got there," he comments as the hairs on the back of my neck stand at attention. I'm stuck in this moment, unable to move. Holding the box firmly to my chest, I slowly turn to look at the stranger.

He's tall and lean, wearing an oversized stuffed

camouflage jacket. As my eyes make their way up his tall frame, I land on his black, soulless orbs. He gives me a creepy smile showing off his crooked teeth. I take a step back, my thighs hitting the car. My body trembles under his dark gaze and I feel the danger radiating off of him.

"Don't move and don't you fucking scream," he commands as his hand slips into his jacket. Still shivering, all I can do is nod. He pulls out a large shotgun with a barrel that looks to have been sawed in half. Without moving an inch, I try to scan the rest of the parking lot for help, but I come up empty.

"Look at me, you bitch. No one is coming to save you," he spits out. His anger rising to a new level. He raises the gun and firmly presses it to my forehead as he lets out a deep menacing laugh. The coolness of the barrel makes a shudder run through my spine. All I can think is *"this is it. This is how I die"*.

With the gun still pressed against my head, he begins again, "Give me your keys and purse. Then turn around and put the box back into the car. Do you understand me? Don't make me paint this lot with your brains," he snarls. Fear races through my body at his words. I juggle the box with one hand as I give over my keys and purse. He snatches them away with a satisfied grin.

"Now the box," he orders as he slowly lowers the gun from my face, still keeping it pointed in my direction. On wobbly legs, I turn my back to him afraid that at any moment he will pull the trigger and end my life. I drop the box back into the trunk and wait for further instructions.

"Now run and hide, little girl. Count to one hundred before you come out." I stand there frozen not wanting to anger him but also not knowing where to go.

"On the count of three I want you out of my sight or I will put this gun to use." My legs are shaking from fear and from cold. *Will I be able to run away?*

"One," he booms from behind me, pressing the gun into my back. My brain is empty. I can't think.

"Two." *This is it.* He's going to shoot me because I don't think I can move. And then it comes.

"Three." My legs move of their own accord as I race through the parked cars. I don't know where I'm heading but I know it has to be far. As far as I can get so he can't find me. It's dark but I don't dare look back. My heel catches in a small hole flinging me forward onto my knees. I don't have time to worry about the pain as I crawl around the car beside me to hide. I begin counting but the numbers become a jumbled mess in my mind. I don't know how long I stay hidden, but I decide to risk it before I freeze to death. Staggering to my feet, I realize the heel is broken on one of my shoes. It must have been the one that got stuck in the cement. Wobbling, I take off toward the entrance to the studio. I can barely see the lights, but I think I'm heading in the right direction. I make my way through the throng of parked cars and finally see the sign for the studio. I pick up my pace, wanting to get safely inside as quickly as possible. My other heel catches on something and again I am being thrown through the air. I close my eyes tightly as I brace for the hard impact that doesn't come. Instead, I'm hoisted up by strong arms and a firm chest. Momentarily, I'm struck with fear that the man has come back to finish the job.

"Let go of me! Get off!" I scream as I try to push away from the body that's clutching me tightly.

"Sarah?" The man questions. I stop fighting and look up at the familiar face. A floodgate of emotions barrels through me at the sight. Tears pour from my eyes and emotion clogs my throat rendering it impossible to tell him what's going on. Travis looks down at me with concern as he tries to comfort me.

"You're hurt," he acknowledges. "Who did this to you?" He angrily questions, tilting my chin up to examine the rest of my body. Travis removes his jacket and places it around my shoulders while I try to find the words to tell him. The immediate heat and his masculine smell seeps into my frigid body, I couldn't be more thankful that someone I trust is here with me.

"Th-there was this man," I start with a sob. "He held a gun to my h-head." I press my hand to my forehead feeling a sticky mess where the rough barrel broke through my skin. "H-he stole my car and purse." I know I'm still in shock and the severity of this situation will hit me soon enough. Travis' jaw is clenched by the time I finish recalling everything I can think of.

"I'm getting the police out here now. Come sit in my truck until they arrive. That way we can get you warmed up. Why are you out here without a jacket, Sarah?" He asks still tightening his jaw.

With chattering teeth, I reply, "I was running out to my car for the box of toys. I didn't think I would be out here this long. Oh no! What am I going to do about the Toys For Tots charity? Those children need those presents! I don't want them waking up on Christmas morning without anything to open," I rush out.

Travis puts his warm hand on my face, gently tilting

my head to look at him, "One thing at a time, Sarah. I promise we won't let those kids go without a Christmas." He opens the truck door and helps me up into the seat. His truck is huge and warm. I sink down into the seat and pull my knees up to my chest as I relive tonight's trauma. My black dress rides up my thighs and I see my bloodied knees full of dirt and gravel. I groan from the pain that begins to seep in. The more my muscles relax, the more I realize how tightly I was holding myself together.

Tears trickle down my cool cheeks and I want nothing more than to be anywhere but here. Fuck. I don't want to go home. The thief can get my information off the items in my glove box. I don't have my phone to be able to call my landlord, or Lizzie for that matter. Although, she couldn't help. Her and Miles left for Savannah, Georgia this morning for the Christmas holidays. This night just keeps getting better and better. *Not.*

I see Travis pocket his phone as he walks around the truck and gets in on the driver's side. "The police will be here soon, along with EMTs to have a look at you. I will get to the bottom of this, I promise you." I nod my head in response and continue going through my options on where I'm going to go tonight. "What's going on in that head of yours?" He questions, pulling me from my thoughts.

"I don't have anywhere to go tonight. I don't want to go home alone, and I don't have my wallet to get a hotel room and Lizzie and Miles are out of town. I don't have anything." I try to stay calm, but the seriousness of my situation is hitting me hard.

"You're coming home with me. I want to make sure you're safe." I open my mouth to argue, but it's quickly closed when he continues, "Don't argue with me, Sarah.

I will carry you over my shoulder if I have to." Police cars with their lights on begin piling into the parking lot. Opening the truck door, I take a deep breath and steel myself for all questions to come.

CHAPTER 1

13 days til Christmas...

Travis

My phone buzzes from the nightstand, illuminating the room. Squinting from the harsh light, I open the message app.

> **Miles:** Something's come up and I need your expert services. Will call tomorrow with the details. Sorry for the late message.

> **Travis:** Just let me know what you need.

I place the phone back down and wonder what Miles has gotten into this time. If he needs my help, then it's something serious. I started my security business right out of the military. It was the main thing I knew how to do, and I did it well. Royal Elite Security quickly became the largest and most sought-after security company in the field. I work with high profile commercial and residential clients who sing our praises day after day. After a dangerous mission overseas went bad and my best friend died in my arms, I vowed to always protect those that I could. I hired my team of ex-military personnel; we work together like a well-oiled machine.

Rolling over, I drift off into a dreamless sleep wondering what Miles needs from me.

◆ ◆ ◆

The phone alarm blares through the room, jarring me awake. Harley, my boxer pup, jumps on the bed to make sure that I'm getting up.

"I'm awake. I'm awake," I mumble to her as she licks my hand trying to get me to pet her. I scratch her head and ears as I pry open my eyes and sigh at the bright light streaming through the window. Groaning, I sit up and swing my legs over the side of the bed. I don't have any notifications from Miles yet, so I get to my feet and head downstairs to let Harley out. She runs in front of me heading straight for the door knowing she is about to play outside. I let her out and head back to my bathroom. I run through today's schedule in my mind as I step into the shower. I stand, letting my head drop as the hot water runs over my body. My mind struggles to wake up. I definitely need coffee. After shaking off the sleep, I step from the shower and begin my morning routine.

I pull on a pair of jeans and throw on a long-sleeved Henley. I'm going to be out in the field installing equipment today so there's no need for me to be dressed in a suit. That's one thing I like about my company, even though it's grown, I'm still able to get my hands dirty. I never wanted to be stuck in an office all day. I wouldn't know what to do with myself.

Once I'm dressed, I go back downstairs to start up the coffee and run through my emails. There's one from my contractor I hired to do some renovations on my house. My bedroom, kitchen, and living room are already complete, but all the spare bedrooms, along with the home gym, are still being revamped. I wanted a house on the outskirts of the city, and this is what I found. It needed some work, to say the least. As soon as I moved in I installed all the best security equipment money can buy, even going as far as to build a fence around the property. It's perfect for Harley and gives me peace of mind knowing that no one can come on to the property and take her.

She comes up to the sliding glass door and whines for me to let her in. I make her wait while I fill her bowls with fresh water and food, then I let her in. She hauls ass to the kitchen and tears into her breakfast. I chuckle at her enthusiasm. I've had her since she was eight weeks old. I needed a companion with me when I retired from the military. She's been the best dog I've ever had.

I pat her on the head as I walk over to the counter and make my coffee. Leaning against the marble countertop, I pull out my phone and see a new message from Miles.

Miles: Call me once you get into the office. I need a full sweep of an apartment and then high-tech equipment installed. Some shit went down last night with my girlfriend and her ex, and he made some threats.

Travis: We will get her taken care of. You don't have to worry about that. I'll call soon.

Miles: Thanks, man. I owe you one.

Fuck, someone messed with the wrong family. The Knight's are like royalty in New York. If this asshat knows what's good for him then he will leave well enough alone. I'll do what it takes to make sure his girl is safe.

I head into the office early to take care of some emails that came through last night. One of my clients had a camera go out on their property so I will send Ryan out there to see what's going on. He's my second in command, if

I can't get to something that needs doing, Ryan is the next go to. I have a feeling I will be busy most of the day with Miles. I check my watch and decide to go ahead and give him a call.

"Hey, man. Thanks for calling me. You're the first person I thought of to take care of this," Miles says when he answers the phone.

"Anything for you man. Tell me what happened," I reply. Miles let's out a deep breath and fills me on what took place last night.

"I went to pick up Lizzie, my girlfriend by the way, I'll have to introduce you. But I went to pick her up from work and her crazy ex was there trying to kidnap her. He told her that he had her apartment surrounded and that if she did anything to draw attention to them he wouldn't hesitate to harm her roommate. Sarah is like a sister to Lizzie, so of course, she went along with what he said," Miles pauses for a moment and then continues, "I got there just in time to beat his ass. When I saw his hands on her, I lost it."

"What a stupid motherfucker. Is your girlfriend alright?" I ask, genuinely hoping that she wasn't harmed in this act of violence.

"She's pretty shaken up, even if she won't admit it. She did end up with a pretty brutal black eye but that was because she got caught in the cross hairs and she connected with my elbow," Miles sighs. I know he is beating himself up about that.

"Damn, I'm sorry to hear that. What can I do for you?" I question.

"Well, since he threatened her roommate, I wanted you to install all the necessary security features possible to keep them both safe. Although, If I have a say in the matter, Lizzie won't be going back to her apartment. I want her living with me so I can make sure she's always safe." Miles declares.

"Well, I can definitely take care of the apartment situation. Do you want to meet me there or send me the address? I'm fine with either," I state, looking down at my schedule for the day.

"Can I send you the address? I need to be here in case Lizzie needs anything. She has a slight concussion," he asserts.

"Sure, that's not a problem. I do have some time this afternoon. Does the roommate know I'll be coming by?" I ask, not wanting to give the woman more to stress about.

"I'll let her know. Thanks for this, Travis," he expresses.

"Miles you've been like a brother to me since college. I'll get that apartment safer than Fort Knox. You don't have anything to worry about," I remark.

"Thanks bro. I'll text you the address when we get off the phone."

"I'll keep you updated." I disconnect the call and place the phone on my desk. Scrubbing my hands down my face, I try to imagine what I would have done in that situation. I hate that he's going through this, but I can at least take some of the load off his plate. Straightening up, I look at the address he sent me. At least it's in a safer part of town than I was expecting.

CHAPTER 2

Sarah

Something startles me awake, I look at my phone to see what time it is. I slap my hand to my forehead, with all the chaos of last night, I forgot to set my alarm for this morning and now I'm running super late. I dash out of the bed, stripping along the way and head straight for the shower. Miles insisted that Lizzie and I stay with him until he makes sure our apartment is safe. I wanted to argue that I was fine, but I figured Lizzie needed me after everything went down with her and Jacob at the restaurant last night. I'm not going to lie, it's nice having a bathroom connected to the bedroom.

After a quick shower, I jump into the black dress I packed for today. Makeup is next but I don't have time to a full face. The bare minimum will have to do the trick. Thankfully my hair has no curl in it whatsoever so it will dry straight. After packing my things back into my overnight bag, I take another look in the mirror. "This is as good as it's going to get," I murmur to myself. I shrug my shoulders and turn off the light. Making sure I grab everything, I dash out of the room and down the stairs.

"Morning. Would you like a cup of coffee?" Miles says from the kitchen. I startle a bit because I didn't see him there. I check my watch noting I don't have time for a cup.

"I actually have to go. I'm running late. How is Lizzie doing?" I ask wanting to make sure she is alright before I leave.

"She's still sleeping but some of the swelling in her eye seems to have gone down a bit." Miles takes a sip from his cup.

"Good. Will you ask her to call me when she gets up? I don't want to call her when she is asleep. I know she needs the rest," I'm pulling my jacket on as I'm saying this. It's supposed to be cold today and snowing by the end of the week. A thrill runs through me at the thought of the first snow of the season. I love this time of the year. Christmas is my favorite holiday.

"Will do. Oh, and Sarah, I have a friend going by your apartment this afternoon to install some security equipment." I turn around with a quizzical look on my face.

"Miles, you didn't need to do that. Our apartment is safe, and we're in a good part of town. There's nothing to worry about." He studies me for a moment before replying.

"Please let me do this for you and her. It's for my peace of mind," he states. I don't have time to argue with him right now, but this discussion isn't over. I can take care of myself. I've been on my own longer than I care to admit, but now isn't the time. I need to get to work.

I nod and turn away from him. Making sure I have all of my belongings, I dash out of his penthouse and into the elevator. I put down my bag while waiting on the elevator and run my hands through my hair. I watch myself in the reflection of the door as I put my gloves on. I shake my head, today is going to be hell if its start is anything to go by. I can't believe Miles went ahead and got someone to come to the apartment today without asking me. I'm independent and I don't need a man's help. I can be as hard headed as they come, but I know what's best for me.

As the doors open to the garage, I blow out a breath. There is no sense in getting upset. I will tell this man when he comes that there has been a mistake, and we don't need anything. With that settled in my mind, I walk to my car and make my way to work.

I love seeing all the shops' Christmas displays. Everyone is all bundled up and running around. My mood improves seeing everyone out with their bright faces and bundles of goodies in their arms. I love the holidays but more than that I love being able to wear my knee-high boots. Boot weather is the absolute best.

I round the corner to my office and pull into the parking garage. I arrive with three minutes to spare. Grabbing my purse, I lock up my car and speed walk to the elevator. I work at Big Apple PR Firm, one of the largest public relations companies in the state. I worked my ass off after college to get where I'm at today.

Stepping off the elevator, I take off toward my office. My assistant, Madison, waves me down before I can step through my door.

"I have some messages for you," she holds up several colored sticky notes.

"Thanks, Madi," I mention as I grab the messages.

"Can I get you anything?" Madison asks as I shuffle through the notes.

"Actually, can you grab me a coffee? I was running late today, and I haven't had my morning dose." I laugh because she has a terrified look on her face.

"I'll go now before your meeting with Michelle Richards." I look down at my watch. I don't have much time to prepare before she gets here. Thankfully, I did her presentation last night before everything happened.

"Thanks," I mumble as I head into my office. Madison quickly comes in with my coffee and places it on my desk. "I appreciate you."

"No problem. I can't have you running around without your fuel." She chuckles as she leaves my office.

I make sure I have everything ready for my presentation. I gather my laptop and coffee and head toward the conference room. My client, Emily Blossom, is an artist who has a large showing of her work next weekend. I've been planning this event for a few months now, and it's finally come down to the wire. Michelle Richards is the art gallery owner and I need to present her with the final details of how everything will be handled next week.

The meeting flew by in a blur. Now I'm sitting at my desk finishing up some reports before I can leave for the weekend. I need to get some shopping done. Of course, I've waited until the last minute to buy presents for everyone. Not to mention, I'm the coordinator for our Toys For Tots Charity in our office.

Glancing at my watch, I decide to ditch work early so I can get some items marked off my to-do list. As I pack up my things, I try to make a mental note of where I need to go first. I decide I'm going to swing by my apartment and change before I go out shopping. I'm thinking some leggings, and an oversized Christmas sweater will look perfect among the other shoppers.

"Madi, I'm heading out early, you can too unless you have something that needs to be finished today. I need to get some things done that I've been putting off," I mention as I walk up to her desk.

"Thanks, boss lady. I think I'm about done with everything that needs to be finished." Madison pumps her fist in the air. "I like it when you decide to take off early. Those times are far and few between." I roll my eyes at her.

"Call me if you need anything," I reply as I walk toward the elevators. I get in and take it down to the garage level. I didn't have a car when Lizzie and I first moved here. We took taxis and Ubers everywhere we needed to go, but when I got the large bonus for my work with Club Vibe, I decided it was time to get a car. We went to several different dealerships until I found the perfect car for me. My new silver Honda Accord SXE is gorgeous and makes me feel like a total boss bitch.

Once I get to our apartment, I pull out my overnight bag and walk inside. I'm holding my phone in my hand, not paying attention to my surroundings as I walk up to the door. I topple over a man that is on his knees inspecting our locks. Terror runs through me that this could be one of Jacob's friends come and finish the job from last night.

I scream and reach into my purse clutching the first thing that I find. "Stop! I have pepper spray. Don't come any closer!" I shout with my eyes closed tight.

A deep masculine laugh booms from the man lying beside me. I crack open one eye and see the most handsome man I have ever seen laughing at me.

"I'm not kidding. I will spray!" I shout, louder than what's needed for this tiny hallway.

"I don't think that will do much damage." He laughs again and my irritation grows until I see the object I'm threatening him with. A fucking tube of lipstick is what I have in my hand. I cover my face with my other hand as the embarrassment grows. I know my cheeks are flaming red at this point.

Embarrassment is quickly replaced with anger, "Who the hell are you? And what are you doing in front of my apartment?" I manage to say as I scootch away from the stranger.

"I'm Travis James, owner of Royal Elite Security. Miles called and wanted me to come by to check out your apartment and install some security features." He gets up from where I pummeled him to the floor and offers me his hand. Tentatively, I slide my hand in his and he pulls me up from the floor.

"Thank you," I murmur. Rearranging my dress and grabbing my bags, I set my eyes back on Travis. He's very tall and muscular. His light brown hair is cut short and very neat as though he were in the military at some point. And his dimples are like beacons to my very soul. His chestnut eyes are watching me check him out and I can feel my cheeks flame with embarrassment for the second time in five minutes.

"Miles mentioned that someone would be by. I got caught up with work and suppose I forgot. I'm sorry for running you over. I didn't hurt you did I?" I find myself checking him out more under the guise that I'm looking for injuries.

"No, worries. I'm fine. You must be Sarah." He holds out his hand for me to shake.

"Yes, sorry. Where are my manners? I'm Sarah," I say as I shake his hand.

"Nice to meet you. Sorry for the confusion earlier." He motions to the floor. "I didn't mean to startle you."

A giggle erupts from me. "I'm sorry I threatened to pepper spray you with my lipstick." I palm my forehead and shrug my shoulders.

"I have to say that was a first for me." He chuckles to himself. "Anyways, Miles wanted to make sure you and his girlfriend are safe in this building. He said there was some kind of an incident last night. It's gotten him in an over protective mode."

"To be honest, he's always in a protective mode with Lizzie. That's one of the things I appreciate about him." Searching for my keys, I unlock the door. "Would you like to come inside so we can talk about this? It's better than the hallway." I motion.

"That works. Whatever makes you more comfortable. I don't want to intrude," Travis remarks. I take that as a yes and open the door, holding it so he can follow me in. I put my things down and lead Travis to the kitchen.

"Can I get you anything to drink?" I ask, grabbing myself a water bottle from the refrigerator.

"Actually, water would be great. Thank you." I slide a bottle over to him and open mine.

"So, what is it that Miles is wanting done? Lizzie is barely here anymore," I growl slightly, showing my frustration with the situation.

"Yeah, he did mention that she's always with him, but I believe he wants you safe as well." Travis opens his water and takes a sip. I roll my eyes at Miles. He thinks he can throw his money around and get whatever he wants. Well, I don't need a security system. Lizzie and I have been living here for years and we've never had a problem.

"Travis, I'm sorry that you had to come out here, but I think I'll be fine. I've never had any trouble before. I just don't think that some boy on a power trip justifies me needing security," I tell him trying not to be a bitch but also not caring how it comes out if it gets him to leave. I want to continue on with my independence.

"With all due respect, you shouldn't take threats lightly," he says with a huff.

"I'm not in the business of cowering to people," I remark.

"Well, I'm in the business of keeping people alive and that's something your friend almost wasn't last night." I gulp loudly as I swallow my water down. I didn't think he was going to punch below the belt.

"You don't play very fair, Travis, but I understand where you're coming from. So, what all are you going to do to my apartment?" I question. I hope my home doesn't end up like one big boobytrap for me to stumble into.

CHAPTER 3

Travis

Sarah asked me a question, but I can't take my eyes off her long enough to answer. Her short blonde hair falls into her face every so often and she wipes it away, focusing her radiant green eyes on me. I want to take a bite out of her pale, milky flesh as I take her from behind. *Fuck, where did that come from?* I've never had such a visceral reaction to such an irritating woman in my life. I try to concentrate on what she asked me.

"I didn't come here to play fair, Sarah. I came here to do a job. One that I intend to see through. I want you to be safe." It surprises me how much that's true. I want this woman protected and I want to be the man that does it. She sucks in a breath at my admission, but I don't let her think about it long before I continue. "There are various different cameras that can be installed outside of your door. But first, I'm going to set up a keyless entry. That way people who don't have the code can't come through. I'll also put sensors on your windowsills that will sound an alarm if they're opened." I make some notes on my phone planning all the equipment that I'll be needing.

"Wow, that sounds like a lot of trouble to go through for Miles' girlfriend's friend. Are you sure he wanted all this?" Sarah asks.

"It's exactly what he asked for. I am the best security company in the state, just let me do my job," I retort. I want her to submit and do as she's told, not keep asking all these questions.

"As you wish, your majesty. I'll be in my room if you need anything. I have to run some errands so if you could hurry up that would be great," she huffs as she leaves the kitchen. Sarah doesn't like being told what to do. That much is clear. I watch her glorious ass shake back and forth as she storms away, slamming her door behind her. She shouldn't have left a complete stranger alone in her apartment. This girl doesn't know the first thing about safety, something she clearly needs a lesson in.

I take a moment to look around the apartment. It's very clean and tidy. She has a Christmas tree up in the corner of the living room and everything on the tree matches the aesthetic of the apartment. Of course it is with the stick Sarah has lodged up her ass. She needs something else stuck in there. *Fuck, why can't I stop thinking about her like that.* She's a pain in my ass already and I haven't even started working yet. She's going to get a bag of coal for Christmas. I take note of the number of windows that I can see. I'll add extra sensors to my list for the windows I can't see. I check to see if everything I need is on the list, then I head for the door making sure to lock it as I leave. I'll have Miles give Sarah my contact information in case she needs something before I see her again.

I make my way down to my truck thinking about the infuriating blonde vixen upstairs. There was something about her that struck a chord with me. I try to put her in the back of my mind as I make my way through the city.

I walk into my office, which has been transformed

into a fucking Winter Wonderland while I was away. There is garland with lights, red and green decorations at every turn, and at the very center a huge Christmas tree adorned with more baubles than you could imagine. Loud holiday tunes stream through the speakers.

"Surprise, bossman!" My team jumps out with smiles on their faces. I have to admit, I never thought to decorate this place. Normally I don't decorate anything, not even my home. It's not that I don't like the holiday, I do. It's having been in the Army for so long, this time of year feels like any other. We didn't get a chance to celebrate it much, especially if we were on mission. And that became the case for many years.

"Damn, guys. How the hell did you get this done so quickly?" I ask as I walk around seeing new decorations on every corner. I don't want to know how much they spent on this. I'm sure it was charged to the company. Not that it matters, we are a billion-dollar company, but I don't see the point in reckless spending on things that aren't necessary.

Damien speaks up first. "We got to work as soon as you left. We knew you would enjoy it, Tank." This was a nickname given to me down range because I'm a fucking tank. My friends call me Tank, but my unit called me Top. I enlisted in the Army because I wanted to be boots on the ground. I achieved the rank of Master Sergent during Operation Enduring Freedom. Being down range really brought us together. We fuck with each other any chance we get.

"It looks like Christmas threw up in here," I mention as I walk around.

"Good. Mission accomplished, bitch," The men in my

squad say in unison.

"Who's ass do I need to stomp because of this shit?" The gang starts pointing fingers and just like I suspected it was Ghost. Jack, the Ghost, joined our ragtag team of misfits a few years ago.

"Sleep with your eyes open, Ghost," I mutter as I walk up to my office. I hear them all laughing and high fiving as I leave the room. At least they left my office space somewhat neutral, except for the wreath on my door.

I sit down at my desk and start typing up the list of items I need for Sarah's and Lizzie's apartment. I have everything I need to go ahead and install the keyless entry, but I'll have to order some of the other supplies needed. Deciding to update Miles, I pick up my phone and call him.

"How's it going, man?" Miles questions when he answers the phone.

"Not bad. I went by the girls' apartment. Sarah is something else, isn't she?" I inquire.

"Well, she's a very independent woman. I knew she was going to push back with this security system. I guess I should've mentioned that beforehand." Miles let's out a laugh.

"A little heads up would have been nice. She tried to pepper spray me, man." We both laugh. I think back to the look on her face when she realized she was holding lipstick instead of a weapon. She needs some lessons in self-defense. What if I had been a thief or something? She definitely wouldn't have been prepared.

"Damn, she's a firecracker. Maybe you could tame her. She's single, you know?"

"Yeah, when hell freezes over, man. She's like a literal ice queen." I wince thinking of what she would do hearing me say that.

"She isn't that bad. You must have caught her on a bad day. Anyways, what about the apartment?" he asks.

"I made a list of everything I need. Some I already have. Everything else will need to be ordered. I decided to install a keyless entry for them. They are safer and can't be easily broken into. I'll write everything up and send it over to you."

"Thanks for doing this. It means a lot," he says.

"It wasn't a problem. I'm happy to do it. Also, can you give me Sarah's contact info so the next time I stop by I can warn her?" I ask with a chuckle.

"Sure, I'll text it to you. Look, Elijah just came in here to remind me of an appointment in ten minutes. I'll talk to you later." Miles hangs up.

I send over the email with everything I want to do with the girls' apartment and he replies back with Sarah's contact information. If I send off a text to Sarah now, she can plan for me to come tomorrow. I might wait to send it in the morning, so she has to make time for me. A laugh bubbles up from my chest. I put my phone aside instead of sending her a text. I wonder what she is doing right now. She drives me crazy, but I still can't help but to find her intriguing.

CHAPTER 4

12 days til Christmas...

Sarah

I scoff as I look down at the text that came through from Travis this morning. He must automatically think I don't have plans today. Albeit I don't, but still. He doesn't need to know that. I drum my phone against my hand trying to come up with a response. I finally give up and text him about shopping.

Sarah: I will be in and out all day today. Christmas shopping and all.

Shuffling to the kitchen, I start up the coffee maker and pull down my favorite Christmas mug. It's a decorated Christmas tree with a red sparkly handle. It makes the holiday blend coffee taste better, in my opinion. Taking my coffee, I light up the Christmas tree and sit on the couch enjoying the view. I pull the festive blanket off the back of the couch and wrap it around myself.

I decorated our tree with colors that matched our apartment. I love using blues and browns on the flocked tree. Under the tree is bare, which reminds me of all the shopping I still have to get done. I have to make another list of everything I need to buy. All the lists I have are taking over my life.

Taking the first sip of coffee, I close my eyes and enjoy the wonderful flavors exploding in my mouth. I wish I lived in a place that celebrated Christmas all year long. My mind wanders to Travis for some reason. He doesn't seem like someone that celebrates this time of year. To be honest, he was kind of grumpy. I don't know what his problem was.

I get up and dress for the day. Red leggings, a black off the shoulder sweater, and of course my boots. I'm just finishing up my makeup when I hear a knock at the door. *Joy*. It must be my grouchy security specialist.

I check the peephole and open the door. "Hello, again," I say as I step to the side to let Travis in the door.

"Good morning. Glad I didn't catch you at a bad time." He grins and places his equipment bags down next to the door.

"Yes, how fortunate. How long will this take?" I ask checking my watch.

"Eh, probably about an hour. I'm just doing the entryway today. The rest of the equipment had to be ordered. So, you will be seeing more of me." He smirks as he not so discreetly checks me out. Ugh, men. Although I can't blame him, I feel hot today.

"Alright well I'll leave you to it." I turn to walk away but I have to offer a beverage. My mother always instilled that decency in me. "There is fresh coffee in the kitchen if you would like some."

"Thank you, I take it black," he mentions as he digs through his bag.

"I didn't mean...ugh never mind. I'd be happy to get that for you," I mutter to myself as I head to the kitchen.

This man is going to be the death of my Christmas cheer! I will not have that!

I return with his coffee and he already has the doorknob undone. Wow, he doesn't waste time. At least I should be able to get some stuff done today.

"Here is your coffee." I stand there with my arm outstretched for a moment before he responds.

"You can just set it down over there, so I don't spill it. Thanks." He motions to the table by the door. I swear my eye twitches by waiting on him. I don't know what his deal is, but he acts like he is entitled to something. This is my damn apartment. I let out a sigh and head to the living room, sitting on the couch I turn on the TV. I scroll until I find the Hallmark channel and settle in with a Christmas romance movie. I barely notice the noise behind me so when he comes and taps me on the shoulder, I about jump out of my skin.

"What the hell? You scared me half to death," I screech holding my hand to my chest, thankful I wasn't holding my coffee.

"I called your name, but you didn't hear me with over this crap that you're watching." He motions to the TV.

"This is not crap. This is a Hallmark movie thank you very much. They may be cheesy, but I still love them," I say with a sharp tone to my voice. "Are you finished with the door then?" I question.

"Yes. I need you to pick a four-digit code so I can program it in. Make sure it's not something that's easily guessed like your birthday," Travis says as he moves around the couch to face me.

I think about it for a moment. It needs to be something both Lizzie and I can remember. "How about my high school graduation year? It's the same for Lizzie so it should be easy to remember." I stand from the couch; my head is level with Travis' shoulders. And that's with heeled boots on.

"That should work. What's the year?" he inquires.

"2015."

"I didn't expect you to be twenty-six. You act older for your age." Travis looks shocked as he moves around the couch toward the door.

"I don't know whether to be offended or not," I say in a huff.

"Don't be," he retorts.

"Well, that's easy for you to say. You didn't just have your age insulted. What are you like forty?" It's the only comeback I could think of off the top of my head. Stupid, I know.

"Close. I'm thirty-five. Nice try though," he replies over his shoulder as he types something into the new keypad on the door. "Sounds like you need someone to teach you some manners."

"I have manners!" I shout. "You were the one that brought up a woman's age. Men aren't supposed to do that."

He finishes tinkering with the keyless entry and comes to tower over me. His closeness makes my pulse race. I can smell his cologne. It's something earthy with vanilla and sandalwood mixed in. He pulls my chin up with his thumb and forefinger, wanting me to look him in the eyes.

"Listen here, kitten. Someone needs to get ahold of that ass of yours and show you who's boss."

I swallow the lump in my throat, but I can't help the warm sensation in my lower belly. "Are you the one for the job?" I ask suddenly not sure of myself.

He lets out a deep chuckle then looks back at me with a flare in his eyes, almost a threat. "If I was the one, you wouldn't sit down for a week with that bratty mouth of yours. I don't think you could handle me," he says with a smirk.

"Oh, I never back down from a challenge. That's how I got to where I am today," I say with a smile.

I try to move away from him but his grasp on me is firm. He looks above us, drawing my eyes in the same direction. The mistletoe. Of course that's what we are under.

"Tell me to stop, Sarah." His words ring through my ears but for the life of me I can't speak. I don't know if I want to speak. Maybe I do want this hot irritating caveman to kiss me. Maybe I want to see what the short stubble on his jaw feels like as he takes what he wants from me. I don't move as Travis' mouth descends on mine. His lips are warm and taste of coffee. There's something electric about the way his lips feel pressed against mine. He runs his hands into my hair pulling gently at first and then harder, the deeper the kiss goes. He licks the seam of my lips and I gasp, allowing his tongue access to my mouth. A moan escapes my lips as his other hand trails down my side and pulls my waist closer to his. I can't get enough of his touch. My hands grasp the fabric of his shirt to pull him closer just as his phone begins to ring.

He pulls away from me and continues to stare into my eyes. He doesn't take them off me until he slides his phone to his ear. I can hear through the speaker that it's a work call. Someone needs some maintenance done to their security system before the snow storm hits later this week. I turn away to give him some privacy. But he isn't having it. He pulls me flush against his hard body as he speaks to the customer on the phone. He hangs up, sliding the phone back into his pocket.

My body tingles at his touch. "That's one way to shut you up. That mouth of yours is something else." I open my mouth to scoff but he catches my lips with his in another scorching kiss. "The lock on your door is finished," he murmurs against my lips. Did he really just say that in the middle of a kiss. This man is giving me whiplash.

I take a step back, looking up at his lustrous brown eyes. I decide to be polite and not ask what the hell just happened. "Thank you for coming by Travis. I suppose you will text me when the other parts come in?" I ask as I take another step back. I need to get away from his magnetism. He nods his head and turns away from me, packing his equipment as he goes.

Is he going to even mention the kiss? Was it only because of the mistletoe that I hung. Maybe I'm a shitty kisser. No, no, no, I'm not going down that road. I am a strong independent woman, and he can't handle it. Yes, that's what I'm going with.

CHAPTER 5

Travis

What the hell was I thinking. Yes, there was mistletoe there but it's not like I have ever participated in that little tradition before. I run my hand through my hair as I drive across town to the office. There's something about that little brat that I find attractive. Of course, she is beautiful but it's more than that. As I'm deep in thought, my phone rings bringing me back to the present. My mom flashes on the screen. I punch the speakerphone button on the steering wheel.

"Hey mom. How are you?" I ask as I navigate through New York traffic.

"I'm doing fine. How are you, my darling?" she questions.

"Everything is great. Business is going well as usual. I have no complaints." I make a right into the parking garage by my building.

"Any girls you want to bring home for me to meet? I'm not getting any younger you know. I want some grandkids before I'm too old to play with them." I roll my eyes. I hear this from her all the time. She's worried about me spending another Christmas alone.

"Mom, not this again. When I meet someone, I'll

let you know. For now, I'm too busy with work and renovations on the house." I try to mollify her, but I know she will keep pressing.

"Son, you work too hard. You need to have some fun every now and then," she protests.

"I go out with the guys after work sometimes. I promise, I'm alright," I insist.

"Fine. I can take the hint. You don't want to talk about this. I just want you to be happy, Travis," she says with a sigh.

"I'm happy mom. I need to go because I just pulled up to the office. I'll talk to you later."

"Alright dear. Love my boy," she croons.

"I love you, too, mom." I hang up the call and rest my arms over the steering wheel. I'm the last one in my family that hasn't settled down yet. I guess I haven't found what I'm looking for. My thoughts go briefly to Sarah and her emerald, green eyes. She's someone I could be interested in. I scoff at myself. She doesn't need an old man like me.

I head into the office and the Christmas music blares from the speakers. I swear it looks more like the North Pole every time I walk in here. I can't put my finger on it, but I know those fuckers are adding decorations every time I'm out of the office. I shake my head. I'll get them back.

9 days til Christmas...

The equipment for Sarah's apartment finally came in. I texted her to let her know, but she hasn't gotten back with me about a good time to come by. I know she read the message so either she is ignoring me or just forgot to respond.

Checking my watch, I decide to go on and head that way. It's almost closing time around here so she should be out of work soon. I collect the security gear and haul it out to my truck. I drive across town, seeing children play in the fresh blanket of snow. It stirs something in my chest that I don't have the energy to reflect on that right now.

I park, grab my things and head up to Sarah's apartment. I knock a few times without any answer. I take out my phone and pull up Sarah's contact information, hitting call. I move my phone away from my ear and hear Sarah's ringing inside the apartment. I knock again with no answer. Something doesn't seem right. She opened my message about an hour ago and now she isn't answering. I stand there and contemplate the implications of putting in her code and making sure she is okay. I go back and forth with myself for a minute until I call again, and she still doesn't answer.

Biting my lip, I put in her code and the door unlocks. I step inside and it feels like a furnace in here. The Christmas tree lights are on and so is the TV. I put my things by the door and walk over to the living room. I don't want to startle her if she's asleep. Walking around the couch, I see a bundled-up Sarah with way too many blankets on for the temperature it is in here. I feel her forehead and I know immediately she has a fever. Sitting on the edge of the couch, I try to wake her but she's too groggy to notice I'm there.

Military training kicks in. I see a thermometer on the coffee table next to her phone that didn't wake her when

I called. Thankfully it's not an oral thermometer, but a tympanic one. I turn it on and place it in her ear until it beeps. Fuck, her fever is 104.5 degrees. I need to get her cooled down. I drag off the blankets that she is bundled under. She still doesn't move. Getting to my knees in front of her, I move the hair from her face.

"Sarah, it's me," I whisper. She moves ever so slightly and her eyes land on me for a moment then close again. I have to take matters into my own hands. I get up from the floor and walk around the apartment until I find the bathroom. Looking behind the mirror, I find some over the counter meds that should help bring her fever down if I can get her to take them.

Grabbing those, I head to the kitchen for a bottle of water. I kick off my shoes at the door when I pass by. I have a feeling I will be here for a while. It's a good thing I went by the house and let Harley out before coming here.

I grab the water from the fridge and walk back to the living room. "Sarah, I have some meds for you to take. You need to wake up and get these in your system." She groans and tries to bring the blankets back up her body, but I hold them steady.

"I'm freezing. I need the blankets, please," she silently sobs. I know she must feel awful.

"Here. Sit up and take these and then I'll make you a bath," I coax but she doesn't open her eyes back up. There is only one thing left to do. I need to get her into a lukewarm bath to bring her body temperature down. Hopefully that will wake her up enough to take the meds.

I start the bath and put the stopper in. Making sure it's at the perfect temperature, I set off to get Sarah. Picking her up from the couch, she hardly moves. She feels too hot in my arms. I set her on the counter in the bathroom, leaning her body against me. I can't worry about preserving her privacy right now. She can yell at me all she wants when she's better.

I unbutton her top and thankfully she has a tank top underneath it. Throwing the discarded shirt to the floor, I contemplate how I'm going to get her out of her pants. I don't want to get all her clothes wet. I pick her back up and shimmy the pants down her legs. I try not to ogle her beautiful body but fuck, I'm a man.

The tub is filled enough that I slowly lower Sarah into the water. It sends a shock through her body, and she screams and tries to fight me.

"Listen to me, you have a high fever that we need to get down. You need to get in this tub for a little while. I won't leave you, I promise," I murmur in her ear. She nods her head and clings to me as I lower her completely into the tub.

"Th-th-this i-is co-co-cold," she stutters and sobs.

"I know, kitten. It's just for a little bit." Sarah pulls her legs up to her chest and lays her head down on them. I take this opportunity to find a towel. Once I get back, I scoop water into my hands and pour it down her back. I check my watch and know that it's been enough time. Too long in here and she could get a chill which would make matter worse.

"I'm getting you out now." She nods as I pull her to a standing position, she leans all her weight into me. I wrap her in the towel then pick her up, cradling her in my arms. I remember which room is hers from when she stormed away from me the first day I was here. I lay her on the bed while I look for clothes. Once I find everything I need, I come back to her. She bundled up on her side with her eyes closed.

"I need to get these dry clothes on you, Sarah," I say in a demanding voice.

She squints up at me, like she is seeing me for the first time since I've been here. She nods. "Okay," she whispers.

"I've got to get the wet clothes off of you first. Lift up." She lifts her arms into the air, and I pull the soaking shirt from her body. I don't know what I was expecting but she is the most extraordinary creature I have ever laid eyes on. She is absolutely breathtaking. Throwing the wet shirt to the floor, I slide on a long-sleeved shirt I found. Now is the real testament of my will, to get these dry panties on her. I gently lay her back on the bed, sliding the towel away. I pull the wet panties from her body and replace them quickly, I also add the plaid pajamas pants I found in the drawer.

Picking her back up, I pull the covers back and set her down in the bed. "Can you take some medicine for me? It will help with your fever." She nods as I collect the wet clothes in my hands. I get the water and meds from the living room and bring them back to her. I shake out a couple tablets and put them in Sarah's hand, giving her the bottle of water as well.

"Drink as much water as you can. I'm sure you're dehydrated." She drinks some then hands me back the water and I screw the cap back on, placing it on her side table. Going back to the bathroom, I get a cool wet rag for her head. As I pass by the thermostat, I turn the heat down some. She doesn't need it this hot in here.

I lay the cloth over her forehead, she snuggles into her blankets and goes right to sleep. I check her temperature again and sigh in relief when I see that it's come down to a manageable degree. I press a kiss to her cheek and turn to leave.

"Please don't leave me. I don't want to be alone right now," she mumbles.

"Okay, let me go get a pillow from the couch so I can lay on the floor." I go to turn around but she stops me.

"No! Please just lay with me, Travis." She opens her eyes a little to make sure I'm doing what she asked. I go to the other side of the bed and slide in behind her. Her vanilla scent envelopes me as I place my head on the pillow. "Thank you for taking care of me," she mutters before I hear soft snores coming from her.

Pulling my phone from my pocket, I text the kid that lives next door to me. I ask him to go get Harley and take care of her for the night. He helps me out from time to time if I have to go out of town and she can't come with me. Billy is a good kid and Harley loves him.

I set my alarm to wake up in a few hours to give Sarah more medicine and then I drift off to sleep.

CHAPTER 6

8 days til Christmas...

Sarah

"Wake up. You need to take some more meds." I hear Travis' voice, but that can't be right. I crack open my eyes and there he is standing in my room. I must be losing my mind. Slowly, memories filter in from last night. I felt so terrible, and he stayed and took care of me. Then I asked him to stay in my bed with me. I put my hand over my face. I'm so embarrassed.

"Don't do that. Here take these," he says as he drops the pills into my hand. I drink the rest of the water because my throat feels like the Sahara Desert. "Good girl. Let me go get you some more water." Travis walks out of the room, I check the time. It's the middle of the night and I still feel like crap. I barely remember yesterday but I know I woke up and couldn't go to work.

Travis walks back in with a Gatorade that I had in the fridge. "Here. This will help hydrate you better. You need to get some more sleep if you can." He hands me the bottle and I drink several large gulps. "Now that you are more coherent, do you want me to sleep in the living room?" he asks. I stare at him for a moment, I truly don't want to be alone. I feel comforted when he's next to me for some reason. I always hate being sick and alone.

"Actually, can you just stay in here in case I need something. I really don't want to be alone. Is that alright?" I inquire as I scrunch the sheets with my hands. I feel nervous that he'll say no. I don't want to make him uncomfortable by sleeping in a bed with almost a complete stranger.

"Of course. Let me get you a fresh wash cloth." He takes the one I put on the nightstand and steps into the bathroom leaving me in shock at how sweet and caring he's being. This is definitely a one eighty from the pompous ass he was being this past week. He comes back into the room with a cool rag and places it across my forehead.

"Thank you," I murmur as I snuggle back down into the blankets. I feel sleep coming and I won't be able to stop it.

"Get some sleep. Your body needs rest to fight off this infection." I hear Travis say before I fall into a deep sleep.

I wake to the smell of something cooking. For a moment, I think Lizzie might be home but then I remember that Travis was here last night taking care of me. *Wait. Why was he even here in the first place? Did I let him in?* I don't remember much about yesterday afternoon. I was out of it.

Throwing the covers off me, I pad to the bathroom. I'm horrified at the person staring back at me in the mirror. My hair is a mess and more than that I have really dark circles under my eyes. My face is red, which I guess means I still have a fever. I splash some water on my face in hopes that it will make me look and feel more alive and less like a walking zombie.

As I walk to the kitchen, I take note of how the living room is straightened up. I know I was out here yesterday, but all the blankets are folded neatly on the end of the couch. The tree is on, and I notice out the window that the snow has started to fall. I take a moment to enjoy the view.

Travis comes up behind me with a cup of coffee. "I didn't know how you liked it, but I figured those sweet creamers in the fridge were yours." A chuckle bubbles up from my throat and I look over my shoulder at his holding my favorite mug.

"Yes, those are mine. I love sweet coffee. Thank you for this. Hopefully it will help me feel less like the dead," I reply as I take the mug from him. I inhale the sweet scent and take a sip. The sugary coffee fills my mouth, and a moan escapes my lips. "This is delicious."

"I made some oatmeal for you with a little bit of brown sugar. I didn't think you needed anything too rich, but you do need to eat something and get back to resting." I follow behind him as we go to the kitchen. I'm shocked to see that he has found my tray and was going to bring me breakfast in bed.

"You did all this for me? You really didn't have to. I would have been alright." I take a bite of the creamy oatmeal, it's just what I needed.

"You were basically unconscious when I got here yesterday. I knocked on the door and called several times. I could hear your phone going off, but I didn't know why you weren't answering. I had a bad feeling, so I used your pin for the door. I'm glad I did. Your fever was high, and you needed someone to care for you." Travis stands straighter behind the counter. He looks like he'd getting ready for a fight. I should probably be mad that he came in like that, but instead I'm thankful.

"I'm not about to yell at you if that's what you think. I'm glad you were able to get to me. I don't remember much from yesterday afternoon. But don't get used to breaking into my apartment." I smile at him over my mug.

He crosses his arms over his chest and the muscles ripple out. I try and fail at checking him out. I feel like he is doing this on purpose. "I was worried about you. I'll do it again if you don't answer the phone or your door." He stands there looking like he is waiting for me to fight back. He has a smile ghosting his lips. *The bastard.* I don't know what I'm going to do with this man.

"Well, maybe I'll have to change the pin number so you won't be able to access it anymore," I taunt. I'm not going to change the pin number. He wasn't creepy coming in here. He was actually worried about me and took care of me. I don't know the last person that was concerned about me, other than Lizzie.

"I wouldn't do that, kitten. Besides, I can override it anyways." A devilish smile spreads across his handsome face.

"What are you going to do, punish me? Isn't that what you said I needed the other day?" I purr feeling myself come alive under his scorching gaze.

"Don't tempt me with a good time. I don't think you know what you're asking for," he says with a smirk.

"Maybe a demonstration is needed. You won't know what's effective until you try a few things to see what puts my inner brat to rest." I'm intentionally goading him now and I can see it in the way his nostrils flare.

"It's good thing you're sick, otherwise, your ass would be on fire for talking to me like that. Finish eating. You need rest," he scolds as he pushes my bowl of oatmeal closer to me.

I eat a little over half of the bowl before I go lay down on the couch. I wrap up in a blanket and turn on the Hallmark channel.

"Ugh, not this again. All these movies are the same." Travis shakes his head at the TV as he takes a seat by my feet.

"They are the best at getting you into the holiday spirit. Lizzie and I used to watch them all the time, especially this time of year." A sad pang hits my heart that that time of my life might be over. She found her man. I couldn't be happier for her, but I wish I could find my Prince Charming. I look over at Travis and wonder what he would be like as a partner. He seems to make a pretty great friend. He stormed into my life and I am already dreading when he is finished installing the security equipment. Then there will be no reason for me to see him. The thought is unsettling and I'm not sure why. It's not like I really know anything about him.

"I don't think these movies will get me in the Christmas spirit," he mentions not turning his eyes from the television.

"No? What does then?" I question.

"Not much really. I never really celebrate this time of year. When I was in the military we often didn't celebrate for whatever reason, and I guess it followed into civilian life. My team that I work with tricked me the other day and decorated the office while I was out. I came back to a

Winter Wonderland explosion. We're always fucking with each other like that." He's looking at me now and I can see the love he has for those men.

"What branch were you in? My dad was in the Army," I mention. I haven't spoken about him in years, but talking to Travis brings up his memory. I just brought him up out of nowhere.

"I was in the Army, as well," he responds lifting my feet into his lap and softly massaging them. I'm so thankful that I'm shaved, and that my toes are painted. I know it's vain, but I hate my feet so I like to try to make them look pretty. "What did your father do in the Army?" he asks.

"He was in COMSEC. He was overseas for four years on his last stint, but he didn't make it home. I was in middle school when the news came." I look back to the TV not wanting to relive that part of my life. I miss my father every day, but I couldn't go through that again.

Travis massages my feet more, taking my mind off of everything. "I'm sorry for your loss. I, too, lost my father at a young age," he mentions.

"I'm sorry. Can we talk about something else? I don't like drudging up the past." I look back to the TV as a silence falls over us.

I start to feel bad again and I know it's time to take some meds. "When was the last time I took medicine?" I don't think I even looked at the clock, I just took them when he handed them to me.

He presses his hand to my forehead, I can feel the heat radiating off me. I know that I have a fever again, or maybe still. It might not have fully gone away to begin with.

"I'll go get you some ibuprofen and then you can nap while I install the rest of your security features. Since you're sick, you can't fight me on what I install." He gives me a wicked smile as he places my feet back on the couch and gets up to get the medicine.

I roll my eyes at him, but he doesn't see me. He would probably say I was being a brat again. He brings the medicine bottle and the Gatorade that was by the bed. He tosses out a few pills and hands them over.

"I'm going to get some work done while I'm here. Then I need to get back home to my dog," he mentions nonchalantly like he didn't just tell me that he stayed here all night when he needed to be at his home taking care of his dog. I nearly choke on my drink.

"Why the hell are you still here when you need to be somewhere else? I can take care of myself. You don't have to stay." I feel terrible.

"I stayed because you asked me to. It's okay, I texted the boy that lives next to me and he went over and picked her up. Everything is fine."

"Oh, God! I asked you to stay? I'm so sorry! Why didn't you just tell me that you had to go?" I put my arm over my face trying to shield my embarrassment.

"You asked me to stay and said you were scared. I didn't want to leave you. You were very sick when I got here yesterday. I would have stayed even if you didn't ask me," Travis says like it's not a big deal. He's done so much for me.

"Thank you, Travis. You didn't have to do this for me. I really appreciate it." He leans over kissing my forehead and then he goes to the door to get his equipment. He treats me like a queen, I can't help but wonder if he likes me or if he is just being the nice guy he is. I ponder this as he tinkers about, until I eventually fall asleep.

I wake some time later and I know it's been a while, the sun is setting in the sky. I look around but I can already tell he's gone. The air feels electric when he is near and it's just my normal apartment when I wake up. I deflate back into the couch feeling sorry for myself. I know he had things he had to get done elsewhere. I mean he can't stay in my little bubble forever. As I look over to the coffee table for my Gatorade, I see a handwritten note sitting there. I hurriedly shed the blankets and grab up the note to read.

Sarah,

Your phone was dead, and I didn't want there to be a chance that you didn't get this message. I'm sorry I left before you woke but I didn't want to disturb you. Your fever was down when I left but take some acetaminophen around two o clock. Everything is installed and connected to the tablet I left there. If you have any questions, don't hesitate to call. Hope you get to feeling better soon.

Travis

P.S. Would you like to grab a bite to eat once you are well?

I squeal and reread the note. Maybe he does like me after all. I clutch the note to my chest. I feel like a schoolgirl tossing my legs up and down in the air. Maybe just maybe this is a date. I fall back onto the couch and smile up at the ceiling.

CHAPTER 7

Travis

I hated leaving Sarah there by herself, but at least I knew she was safe. There's no one getting into that apartment. I just hope she gets well soon. I make a quick stop at Billy's house to pick up my pup, they are outside playing when I pull in. As soon as I stop, Harley comes sprinting toward me, jumping right in the truck.

"Thanks for looking after her, Billy, especially on such short notice. There was someone I was helping," I state.

He comes up to the truck. "Not a problem, Mr. James. I love having her over here." He pets her goodbye and I hand him some cash. He used to always try and decline the offer until I told him I wanted him to have it. Now, he takes it and thanks me.

Once we're home, I pour Harley some food and refresh her water bowl. She runs off to her bed and starts chewing on a toy, leaving me in her wake feeling like something is missing. I scratch my beard and realize that I miss Sarah. Even with just the little time we spent together, I got used to being around her. I look around my home and wonder what she would see. She would probably have a fit that I don't have a Christmas tree up. I laugh to myself as I head up to my room to get a shower.

Throwing my clothes into the hamper, I jump into the shower. I love the feel of the hot water cascading down my back. Images of Sarah flash in my mind and my cock springs to attention. *Her stunning green eyes looking up at me while she's on her knees before me. She wraps her perfect rosy lips around my cock, taking me all the way back into her throat. Tears stream down her cheeks as I fuck her face faster and deeper. I grab a handful of her silky blonde hair as I continue to thrust into her mouth. She moans and the vibrations feel amazing along my shaft. She cups my balls with her hand and massages them as I pound away.* I feel the tingle at the base of my spine and within seconds I'm coming jets and jets down the drain, wishing Sarah was here to swallow me down. I haven't had this kind of reaction to a woman in a long time, and it's never been this visceral.

I lean against the wall of the shower knowing I need to see her again. I hope she agrees to dinner with me because whether she likes it or not, Sarah's *mine*.

That realization hits me right in the chest. I run my hands through my wet hair as I step out of the shower. I know one thing for sure. I'm going to have to get that little vixen under control. She may not think she needs anyone, but Sarah will soon find out that she needs me.

I find that she texted me when I was in the shower.

Sarah: Thank you for caring for me, Travis, I would love to grab something to eat with you.

A devilish smile crosses my face as I read through the message. I have a date to plan.

Travis: How are you feeling?

Sarah: I feel much better, actually. I took the meds like you suggested. I think I'll be able to head back to work tomorrow.

Travis: That's good to hear. Would you like to plan to meet up after work?

Text bubbles appear then disappear. Then she finally responds.

Sarah: I have plans to go Christmas shopping, but we can plan something before. I really dropped the ball this year and haven't gotten my shopping done already.

Travis: You still have plenty of time.

Sarah: I guess so. It will just get busier and busier as the days go on. I don't really care for crowds so hopefully I can knock it out in one night.

Travis: I'm sure you can. I'll text you the details tomorrow.

Sarah: I look forward to it.

I place the phone on my dresser as I pull out some sweats to wear for the rest of the day. I called the office and told them something came up so there isn't anywhere I need to be. I can just hang around here and maybe get some work done on those spare bedrooms. The renovations crew is here so I might as well offer my services to get this job done faster.

For the rest of the day, I get lost in manual labor. It's been a while since I've done anything this strenuous, with the exception of working out every day. It feels good to get my hands dirty. It almost feels like I'm back in the Army, just without the harsh conditions.

Once the crew calls it a day, I head downstairs to let Harley out. There is a little snow on the ground which she will love. She's that crazy dog that jumps around in it. She even tunnels her way under it completely when there is more of it.

She sees me coming and races over to the door, bouncing up and down, waiting to be let out. As I open the door, Ryan calls. He's normally able to handle everything on his own, so if he is calling there is a problem somewhere.

"Ryan, what's up?" I question wanting to get down to the problem.

"I was checking all the monitors before I left for the day, and it seems that the new unit you put in for Miles Knight isn't working properly. The door lock doesn't seem to be online. I rebooted the system, but it still says there's an error. Would you like me to go over and take a look?" He asks. That's Sarah's door he's talking about, I'll be damned if another man goes over there except for me.

"No, I'll go have a look. Thank you for letting me know. Anything else?" I'm hoping that's all because I need to get to Sarah's apartment to make sure she's safe. I'm already pulling on my shoes and opening the door to let Harley back inside. She comes flying through the door and skids to her water bowl in the kitchen.

"I'll be back, girl." I scratch behind her ears as she perks up, knowing that I'm leaving.

I jump in my truck and make my way across town. I texted her before I left but I haven't heard anything. She needs to be better at responding or I will end up at her place more often than not just to check on her.

I pull into the parking lot for her building and cut the engine. I pull my bag of tools from behind my seat and head up to her apartment, nearly knocking over a caroler on the way.

"Sorry ma'am. Sorry." I yell back as I make my way up the stairs. *What the hell is wrong with me? I almost took out an old lady singing Christmas carols in an effort to get to Sarah.* I round the corner and jog to her apartment door which is thankfully closed. Leaning down to check the device I hear something that can only be described as the sound of dying cats screeching out. Twisting the handle, I open the door to a sight that will be permanently seared into my mind.

Sarah is in a pair of pale purple satin shorts with a matching tank top. She has mismatched Christmas socks that go up to her knees, but that's not the part I'm concerned about.

Sarah has a hairbrush in her hands and is belting out a Christmas song. I think it's that one by Mariah Carey that people go crazy over every year. She is absolutely carefree and stunning as she dances about and sings.

"I don't want a lot for Christmas.

There is just one thing I need.

Don't care about the presents underneath the Christmas tree.

I don't need to hang my stocking there upon the fire place.

Santa Claus won't make me happy with a toy on Christmas day.

I just want you for my own.

More than you could ever know."

She squeaks out. I think under normal circumstances she would sound okay but with her having been sick, she sounds like a frog. I can't help but to sit here in awe and laugh at this side of her that I've never seen.

She shakes her ass and slides around the floor on her socks singing along with the loud music. It isn't until she turns her sassy self around that she sees me there smiling at her. The pure shock and embarrassment on her face isn't one that I'll soon forget. She drops the brush from her mouth and rushes to her phone to stop the music. When she looks back up her cheeks are rosy, probably from the exercise and the embarrassment.

"Wh-what are you doing here, Travis?" She asks a bit out of breath.

"I came because your door unit is showing that it's offline, so it's not working. Did you have a blip in power today?" I question.

"I, um, yeah actually. The power surged for a moment, but it came right back on." Sarah remarks trying to cover her chest from view. She picks up a throw blanket and drapes it around her body. I wish I wasn't making her uncomfortable.

"That's what happened then. I can show you what to do next time that occurs. I promise I'm not making it a habit of just coming inside your door. I did text you to let you know I was on the way and then I heard you singing, and I had to see that for myself. I'm sorry for making you uncomfortable." I say averting my eyes from her.

"Sorry I didn't see your message or hear it come through. I guess I was a little preoccupied." She blushes and wraps the blanket tighter and comes to stand next to me.

"You need to be more conscious of your surroundings, Sarah. I understand you didn't know about the lock, but anyone could have gotten in here. I guess I'm just paranoid from the military." I reply ruefully.

"Well, you didn't mention there would be a problem if the power went out. This is all new to me. I also didn't ask for this if you remember. I think keys are just fine." She bites out as she gestures to the door.

"It's the nicest keyless model there is. I just wanted to make sure you were safe. My second in command called me at home to tell me something was wrong. I'll reboot it and get out of your hair." I open my bag and get the small pin I use to press the reset button. "I'll leave this with you in case this happens again. All you have to do is press this small button and then the prompts will tell you what to do." I go through the steps for her to see and then hand her the small pin. I zip up my bag and turn to leave.

"Since you are here, I was going to order something for dinner. Would you like to stay and watch a movie? I can't promise you will enjoy the movie," she says with a quirk of her lips. I don't even have to think twice.

"I'd love to." I drop my bag and close the door.

"I'm going to go change. Is there anything you are craving?" She asks as she heads to her bedroom. *Nothing but you* I think to myself. Tonight is going to be torture. I feel like I've definitely been friend zoned at some point. I must be too old for her. I don't feel too old, but who knows what she's thinking.

"I'm good with anything. I'm not picky." *Except when it comes to you.*

CHAPTER 8

8 days til Christmas...
Sarah

I change into some flannel jammies and comb my fingers through my hair. I'm not going to add makeup because he's already seen me without it several times. He's actually seen me at my worst when I was sick. I looked like death. I hear him call out that he doesn't care what we have for dinner, so I guess I have to decide. Walking out in the living room, I see him still standing close to the door looking uncomfortable.

"You can sit you know. I'm not going to make you stand through dinner and a movie." I chuckle as I go to the kitchen to get my assortment of take-out menus.

"It's not polite to be seated unless invited to do so," Travis states.

I bring the menus out and slap him in the stomach with them. "You have slept here already. You come when you please. You aren't a guest anymore. Now, we won't ever eat if you make me chose so you had better make the decision." He lets out a chuckle as I leave him there and walk over to the couch and plop down. He follows along and sits at the other end. I guess this is a friend dinner. I mean of course it is. We don't really know anything about each other. But he doesn't seem keen to be seated next to me. Like I might bite or something.

Travis shuffles through the menus until he gets to Thai Palace. It's one of my favorites and I'm secretly hoping he picks that one.

"How about this one? Thai sounds good to me." I inwardly jump for joy.

"Great, that's what I was hoping you would pick," I reply with a fist pump in the air.

"If you knew what you wanted then why did you make me pick?" he asks with a baffled look on his face.

"I don't know. I didn't know what I wanted until you flipped to that page then I was hoping you would pick it. It's a girl thing. We can't decide shit." I shrug my shoulders as he laughs at me. I laugh along with him, it just feels right. Him being here seems normal, easy. Maybe we'll be just friends. There isn't any pressure then.

We order our dinner and he insists on paying, which I argue with him about for several minutes. When I finally give up, I turn on the TV so we can pick a Christmas movie.

"Are there any Christmas movies that are your favorite?" I ask as I scroll through Netflix. I know he doesn't want to watch a Hallmark movie. He would probably take his food and leave if I turned one on.

"I guess White Christmas with Bing Crosby is one my all-time favorites. We used to watch that when I was little. They also played it the first year I was in the military." He looks over at me with nostalgia in his eyes. It's not my favorite but I don't hate it and it just so happens to be on Netflix.

I queue up the movie and turn to Travis. "White

Christmas it is then," I say before pressing play.

"We don't have to watch this. We can watch whatever you'd like," he replies.

"No, that's okay. I haven't seen this one in a while." I curl up in my blanket my with legs crisscrossed on the couch. "You know you can get comfortable if you want. You don't have to sit there like a statue. Take your shoes off and stay a while," I joke. He shakes his head at me with a smile on his face. I don't think he knows what to do with me. He listens though and slides his shoes off.

"Can I get you something to drink? Water, tea? I think we have beer and I know some red wine, possibly eggnog." I should have asked sooner. Terrible hostess award goes to me.

"That's quite an assortment you have there," he chuckles, "I'll take a water," he replies. I pause the movie and hop up. I grab two bottles of water and head back to the living room. Before I sit, someone knocks on the door. "It's probably our dinner. I'll get it." I place the waters down and pad toward the door only to be thwarted by Travis. He looks through the peephole then promptly opens the door to grab our dinner. Instead of arguing, I head to the kitchen to get plates and napkins.

"I just wanted to make sure it was the delivery guy. Old habits, ya know?" Travis mentions as he places the food on the table before us.

"No problem. Here's your plate, dig in." I press play and we binge our Thai food while we watch White Christmas. Once we are both full, we cast our plates aside and sprawl out on the couch. We are much closer now but still not touching. I don't know what to make of our situation. Maybe it's all in my head, but some days it feels like we are more. He's so concerned about my safety, maybe that's just from the military training and his line of work. I can make an argument for almost anything involving him. *So, who knows?* It's not like I *need* a man in my life right now. I am so close to making partner in our PR firm. I need this weekend's art show to go off without a hitch.

The movie finishes and I'm not sure how I managed to stay awake through the whole thing. I am bone tired. I imagine it's from the sickness leaving my body. Travis helps me clean up and put away the leftovers.

Walking him to the door I say, "I had a good time tonight. Thank you for coming to check on me again. I guess I need to stop getting myself in compromising positions," I say with a chuckle.

He leans in and my breath hitches. He slides a piece of hair behind my ear and my heart drums in my chest. "I'll be there to make sure you're safe. All you have to do is call me and I'll come," he murmurs as he kisses my forehead and walks out the door. "Make sure you lock this." I nod standing there stunned in the doorway. His lips always send shivers through me. It's unlike anything I've ever experienced before.

"Be safe going home. Oh, are we still on for tomorrow since we technically had a bite to eat tonight?" The question has been churning in my mind most of the night. I didn't know if he would still want to go out.

"Of course, kitten. I'll let you know the plans tomorrow." He gives me a wink and then he's gone, leaving me there trying to figure out what the hell is going on. I shut the door and make sure I lock it before I head to my room for bed. Before I can drift off to sleep, I rehash the whole night, smiling at times but wondering what the heck we are.

CHAPTER 9

7 days til Christmas...

Travis

"There is a large snow storm heading toward the city this weekend. Roads will likely be closed until snow ploughs are able to get through. People living on the outskirts of the city need to take precautions and plan ahead. Grocery stores are already getting hit hard with people stocking up. The snow could last all the way to Christmas Day! That's for all those children hoping for a white Christmas. Everyone stay safe out there. Tune in for more information about the Great Snow Storm of 2022 to come at 11 p.m.," the newscaster says as I turn the TV off. Great, the roads leading into the city will be mainly blocked off if this storm is as large as they say it will be. I love the quiet life away from the city, but this kind of weather makes living on the outskirts hard.

I sip on my coffee as I look out my office window. I can already see the dark clouds rolling in. This thing might hit before the weekend even gets here. I make a mental note of things I need to pick up from the store on the way home this afternoon. I'm not worried about power going off, I have a generator and a fireplace in my home. However, most of the people in New York City don't have that luxury. This kind of storm can be very damaging for the city.

Placing my coffee down, I call in Ryan. His office is a

few doors down from mine and we need to get on the same page in case the power to our building goes out. Someone has to be here to man the generator to keep the people that have our systems connected. However, that's only if they remain with power as well.

Ryan walks through the door and sits in front of my desk. "You wanted to see me, Tank?" he asks.

"Yes, have you heard about this storm that's supposed to hit this weekend?" I question.

"Yes, sir. I heard it on the news this morning before I came in. Are we mandating that someone stay here to run the generators? I volunteer, sir. I already began getting the apartment suite ready for someone to stay in," he mentions. When we bought this building it had an apartment attached to it. Since then, we have used it for various things, one of which being if there was a storm. Someone needed to stay here to make sure the building had power.

"Good work. Go to the store and make sure you have all the food and drinks you need for about a week just to be prepared. This thing could go on longer than they are forecasting. Crank up the generators and check how much fuel they have. You'll need to get some of that as well. Use the company card for whatever you need. Thank you for volunteering. I would have done it myself if it had not been for you," I reply. "Go ahead and take the rest of the day off to get prepared. I'll have one of the other guys take over your schedule today."

"Thanks boss. I'll keep you updated." Ryan stands and leaves just as quickly as he came. With that under control I can breathe a little easier. Our clients depend on us, and I don't want this building to be without power for more than five minutes, tops. Ryan is my second in command for a reason, he was already preparing for the weekend.

I down the rest of my coffee and dive into reports that have needed to get done for a couple days. Once I finish with those, I check my watch. I've got to make plans for tonight and let Sarah know so she can plan accordingly.

Travis: Since you have to go Christmas shopping tonight, do you want to eat someplace close to where you will be going?

I don't have to wait long for her to write back to me.

Sarah: That would be great. I was going to go to the Galleria. They have everything under one roof so would only have to make one trip.

I cringe at the words. I hate that mall. The security is terrible, and the parking lot is dark at night. Definitely not a safe place for a woman to be going by herself.

Travis: How about we eat there then. That way you won't have to drive there in the traffic.

Sarah: Are you trying to go Christmas shopping with me?

Travis: Well, someone has to hold all your bags.

Sarah: Deal, on one condition.

Travis: And what would that be?

Sarah: You have to sit on Santa's lap and get your picture taken.

Travis: That's a negative.

Sarah: Then I guess you won't be coming with me.

I place my phone down on my desk. She's infuriating. I don't want to sit on some old man's lap where I'm sure a hundred kids have peed and then have photographic proof that I did it. *No. No. I won't do it.* Sarah needs to know that she can't boss me around. The bossing is my job. I have seen and done things that would shock her. This little brat needs a reminder of who's in charge, I pick my phone up and write out another text.

Travis: Oh, I'm coming with you, and you know what I said about you needing to get rid of that bratty mouth? Well, you might be getting that punishment sooner rather than later. Is 6:00 good for you?

She reads the message but doesn't respond back to me right away. I didn't expect her to. She has too much pride to be handled by a man. But she has another thing coming if she thinks she can boss me around. I am the boss, and she's about to find out how seriously I take that role.

Sarah

Travis: Oh, I'm coming with you, and you know what I said you needed to get rid of that brat? Well, you might be getting it sooner rather than later. 6:00 good for you?

I reread the message over and over again. I don't know what to respond to that. I don't know if he's playing or if he really wants to spank my ass. I have to admit the thought gets me all hot and needy. I've never been with someone so dominant before, not that I'm with him, but he makes it sound that way. A blush creeps up my face as I reread the message again. I can't believe he said that. *What should I reply?*

I'm interrupted from my thoughts when Madison knocks at my door. My face must show my guilt. "Okay, spill. Who is this mystery man. I saw you messaging back and forth and smiling and now you're blushing. I need all the details." She plops down on the leather chair in front of my desk and eyes me until I start to speak.

"Okay, okay. His name is Travis. I met him last week when Miles sent him to our apartment to install some extra security stuff since everything that happened with Lizzie a week ago," I say.

"Alright, and have you been out yet?" She asks.

"Well, not technically. I met him Friday when I left early from work and we didn't really hit it off, I didn't want the damn security crap in the first place, but it was at Miles' insistence. Lizzie hasn't even been home since then, but that's neither here nor there. So, he comes back the next day to install this keyless lock thingy and he pulled me into the most passionate kiss I've ever had. But I think it was only because we were standing under the mistletoe that I hung. He might just be a good kisser, right?" I question.

"OMG, tell me more!" Madi insists.

"Well, then he left me all hot and bothered. And I didn't hear from him for a couple days since he was waiting for the rest of the equipment he ordered to come in. So, he came over on Tuesday and that's the day I was so sick, remember? Well, he came into the apartment, and I was basically comatose. He took care of me all day and night. I apparently asked him to stay with me and he slept in my bed. Nothing happened of course, but then he made me breakfast the next day. Meanwhile, I still don't really know what's going on," I finish. She sighs and falls back in her chair.

"Sounds like he has the hots for you. My boyfriend

hardly takes care of me when I'm sick. He just throws me a box of cold medicine and leaves because he doesn't want to catch it." She shrugs her shoulders, but I can see the sadness there. Maybe we shouldn't talk about this anymore. "So, tell me what else has happened." She smiles eagerly at me.

"Well, he came over last night to tell me that the thing he installed on the door wasn't working. He could see it from his company computer, so he came and checked on me. But he found me dressed in skimpy pajamas dancing around the apartment and singing to All I Want for Christmas by Mariah Carey. I almost died from embarrassment." I place my hands over my face for a moment. "But he just laughed and stayed for dinner and a Christmas movie. There was no snuggling, no kissing, nothing. I walked him out and he kissed my forehead before he told me to lock the door behind him. I think I have been friend zoned," I admit.

"Oh girl! You can't really think that! He has gone through all this trouble for you. Maybe he doesn't know where your head is at with this whole situation. He sounds like a gentleman. What does he look like? I have to know!" she exclaims. I laugh right along with her.

"Well, he's almost ten years older than me but he's still so handsome and he's really tall like 6'2 or 6'3. He was in the military, so he has muscles for days and the most beautiful brown eyes I've ever seen. He has light brown hair that is cut short on the sides and a little longer up top. He's strong enough to carry me because he did the night I was sick. He put me in the tub to get my fever down. And then we have been texting today because we are supposed to get a bite to eat before I go Christmas shopping, but he acts like he is coming shopping with me. I don't know what to say,"

I admit.

"You say hell yes! Sounds like the man of your dreams, Sarah. Why aren't you going for it?" she asks. I don't really have an answer. I can make all the excuses I want to about not needing a man right now or that he's not really interested but I don't think that's the case. Maybe I'm just scared.

"There is also something that he has mentioned twice now. He's called me a brat and said I needed to get a punishment where I wouldn't be able to sit down for a week," I cover my face with my hands as I feel the blush creeping back up my cheeks.

"Girl! I'm about to text him from your phone that you will do whatever he wants. Sounds like he's a dom. I dated one once and it was the best sex I've ever had in my life." She squeals and I have to look around the office to see if anyone is listening to us. How mortifying would that be.

"So, what? He's like Christian Grey? I don't know if I can handle all that," I murmur as I pull my hands from my eyes.

"He might just like being in control. And there is nothing wrong with that. Trust me. Plus, if there's anything you don't like you can just say stop. And that's that. I say go for it girl." Madi stands and gives me a hug. "I'm excited for you and I can't wait to hear more about him." She smiles as she leaves my office.

I look back down at my phone and reread the message he sent.

Sarah: 6 is perfect. I'll meet you at the entrance to the Galleria.

Butterflies erupt in my stomach after I press send. I don't know how this is going to go but I'm jumping in head first.

CHAPTER 10

Travis

I check my watch and see that it's 5:56 p.m., Sarah should be here any minute. When I look up, she's heading right for me with a smile on her face. Punctual, I like that.

"How are you this evening?" I ask as she walks right up to me.

"I'm great. Coming straight from work but I made it in time. How are you?" She questions as I help her slide off her jacket.

"Better now. So, where to first? Are you hungry now?" I inquire gathering our jackets in my hands.

"I want to do some shopping first. I had a later than normal lunch. Is that okay with you?" She looks up at me from under her long lashes and I want to pull her closer to me. I want everyone to know she's with me and that she's mine.

"Lead the way." I motion for her to go so we can get this shopping over with.

"I need to get some presents for the Toys For Tots charity that my company is sponsoring this year. So, we need to go to the toy store."

"That's a great charity. Let me guess, it was your idea and you're in charge of it?"

"How did you know that?" she asks.

"I had a feeling. You seem like a giver, so it was just an assumption." I shrug my shoulders and give her a wink.

"So, you think you know me or something?" she asks.

"I'm getting there." I hold the door open for her at the toy store. We spend about two hours selecting all kinds of toys for different age groups of children. We have two carts and Sarah has the brightest smile on her face the whole time and keeps throwing more and more items into them. I'm sure she wishes she could see their bright faces on Christmas day. Hell, even I wish that. We will be making some children very happy this year.

Once we are finished at the toy store, we make a trip out to Sarah's car to deposit all the bags before heading back inside.

"I'm starving! All that shopping worked up an appetite. What do you want to get for dinner? The food court has pretty much anything," she remarks.

"How about Charlie's? They have the best cheesesteak sandwiches!" I state. I haven't had one in years, but I remember how good they were.

"Oh, that sounds delicious, lead the way." Her smile lights up her whole face, making me not want to look at anything else. I lead her by the small of her back and the action feels intimate. I wish I was touching other parts of her. She hasn't given me any indication that this is more than just a friendship to her. I groan at the thought of letting her slip through my fingers.

As we eat, we discuss an assortment of interesting tidbits about ourselves. She's an only child from Savannah,

Georgia and her favorite color is teal. She loves the beach and Christmastime. Lizzie is like a sister to her, and they have been best friends since grade school. Sarah truly is one of a kind and I yearn to know deeper things about her.

I have to admit that being here with her is putting me in the holiday spirit. I didn't think it was possible, but here I am wanting to buy her something and put it under the nonexistent Christmas tree that I have in my home. I cringe when I think about how she would react to my bare home. There isn't a trace of Christmas anywhere in it.

We begin walking to the exit of the Galleria and Sarah stops in front of a display of snow globes. "I had one just like that when I was a child. My father gave it to me when he got home from one of his many deployments. I always kept it close to me especially after he passed away. There was one night that my mother drunkenly stumbled into my room, she tripped and smashed it. I think I cried for days because it was the last thing I had of him. My mother took it very hard when my father didn't come home from his last deployment. She began drinking more and more until she eventually passed away from liver failure." Sarah paused for a moment, not taking her eyes off the snow globe in the window. "Dad said that I could shake it anytime I wanted, and it would be like we were together in that little winter wonderland." She looks longingly at the snow globe with a father and child holding hands in the snow looking up at the Eiffel Tower. A faint tear slips down the side of her cheek, so I reach up to wipe it away.

"Sorry, I didn't mean to get upset I just haven't seen one like that in over ten years." She shakes her head as she composes herself. Always acting like what's expected of her. I'm glad I finally got a glimpse behind the curtain.

"You don't ever need to apologize to me about something like this. Do you want to go in the store and look at them?" I ask.

"No, that's okay. I really need to get going. Plus, I have all these other bags that I need to get out to the car." She utters looking down at her hands.

"Let me get those for you. You don't need to carry all that." I take some of the bags from her hands and I see the red indents where the bags were cutting into her. I should have taken these sooner. I'm such a jackass.

After we stuff the bags into her trunk, she reaches into her purse but shuffles her hand around while her eyes stay locked on mine. Taking a step closer to her, I pin her against the car caging her body in with mine. As I run my fingers over her cheek and down to her jaw, I pull her face up to meet mine. We are a breath away and I know I need her mouth on mine. There isn't mistletoe this time, but I don't care. I need this. I need her.

"Tell me to stop, Sarah." She shakes her head as my lips crash down on hers. She lets out a small gasp allowing me access to the rest of her mouth. One hand grasps her waist while the other holds her neck in place not letting her get away from me. Her vanilla and peppermint perfume fills my mind as I dive deeper and deeper within her. My hand threads through her hair pulling her head back further to give me better access. Her sweet lips taste like the warm mocha she just had, I find myself pushing my body further into hers. Sarah drops her purse to the ground and clutches my jacket in her hands, a soft moan escapes her lips and I swallow it down..

Snow begins to fall around us like we're in our own

little world. Pulling back, I push the hair from her face and look into her emerald-green eyes.

"You're absolutely stunning, do you know that? Inside and out," I kiss her again. "I can't get enough of you." She opens her mouth to speak but I pull her in close as a shiver runs through her body. She rests her head on my chest, I take advantage by kissing the top of her head.

"I'm glad you came with me tonight. I wouldn't have enjoyed it nearly as much had I been on my own," she murmurs against my chest.

Larger chunks of snow begin to fall faster, and I know I need to let her go so she can get home safely.

Cupping her cheeks I whisper, "I wouldn't have been anywhere else. We need to get out of here before the snow restricts our vision of the road." Sarah nods and picks up her purse from the ground. I open the door for her but before she slips in she pulls my head down to meet her lips once more.

"Message me when you get home. I want to know that you made it safely."

"I will." She starts her car and leaves me standing there watching after her. Fuck, I've got it bad. That little vixen has me all tied up inside. Once I get to my truck, I blast the heat and head across town for my home thinking of Sarah the whole way.

Once I reach my house, I cut the engine and realize I have a missed text from Sarah. My heart drums in my chest hoping that she made it home safely.

Sarah: Thank you for a wonderful night. I'm home and just to let you know the door is locked and secure.

That little smart ass. I chuckle when I reread her message.

Travis: I glad you are locked safely into your apartment. I just got home myself.

Sarah: I'm glad to hear it. The snow was really falling down.

I ponder what I want to write to her. I need her to know that I want something more than just a friendship. The words don't come to me.

◆ ◆ ◆

6 days til Christmas…

Sarah

The work day goes by slowly, Travis and I spend most of Friday texting back and forth. I invite him to the gallery show tomorrow and he accepts. I think this is turning into something real and I'm as excited as I am nervous. I wish I had my best friend here to talk to, but she and Miles have already left to spend Christmas with Lizzie's family.

I don't have time to plan anything with Travis for today since I have to make sure everything is ready for the event tomorrow. I will be working late into the night. If it goes as planned, I'll be up for partner in the firm. I've worked my ass off the last three years for this position and I deserve it more than anyone here. Better me than Vivian. She tries to take my ideas and run with them but not this time. This exhibit is my baby, as was Club Vibe.

I have more than earned my spot at the top. I just hope everything goes as arranged. But you know what they say about all the best laid plans…

CHAPTER 11

5 days til Christmas...

Sarah

Saturday is finally here. I'm excited and nervous to be hosting this event. I have been putting this art show together for months, tonight it will finally pay off. I invited Travis tonight to come and see the work that I do, he said he would be here, so I definitely dressed for the occasion in my little black dress. You can't go wrong there.

    I get to the studio early to make sure everything is set up correctly. The paintings have already been hung according to the artist's specifications. I just need to make sure all the decorations are how I envisioned them. I want this to be perfect. The caterers are already here getting champagne into all the glasses as Emily, the artist, goes around to make sure all the paintings are perfect. This is her showing and I know she is nervous, so I gave her a bit of a peptalk earlier. I know I'm missing something but I'm not sure what it is until I see the Christmas tree in the corner without the children's gifts under it. Guests had to buy tickets to this event as well as bring a present for Toys For Tots. I left the box with the presents donated at the office in my car. I check my watch and know I have enough time to run out there. I forgo my jacket even though there are snow flurries in the air. I'm just going to run to my car and come right back inside. Getting my jacket from the back would take away precious time that I don't have to waste.

Rushing out of the door, I'm momentarily frozen in place by the cold wind. The snow storm is going to start any minute. I just need to get to my car and back inside before I turn into a popsicle. I look across the parking lot at the man staring at me, an eerie feeling slides over my body leaving goosebumps in its wake. Travis told me I needed to be more conscious of my surroundings, but now it's too late. I can feel him closing in on me and there is no way to escape. The predator caught it's prey and the prey is me.

I fly into Travis' arms, my emotions clog my throat once I realize I'm safe. Tears spring from my eyes and down my cheeks as he demands answers from me.

"What the hell happened to you? You're hurt, Sarah! Who did this to you? I'm going to find them and put a fucking bullet though their fucking skull." His anger radiates off of him making me tense. "I'm sorry, baby. Take deep breaths. In and out. In and out. Good, just like that." He holds me close against his body, opening his jacket and enveloping us both inside. His cologne fills my lungs and makes the tension in my body loosen to some degree.

"Th-there was this man," I start with a sob. "He held a gun to my h-head." I press my hand to my forehead feeling a sticky mess where the rough barrel broke through my skin. I'm sure I look like a mess, but I have zero fucks left to give. They flew out of me the moment I took off through the cluster of parked cars. "He stole my car and purse." I know I'm still in shock and the severity of this situation will hit me soon enough. I tell him everything that happened, and Travis' jaw is clenched by the time I finish recalling everything I can think of.

"I'm getting the police out here now. Come wait in my truck until they arrive so you won't be so cold. Why are you out here without a jacket, Sarah? Damnit, you're freezing!" He exclaims as he runs his hands along my arms. I shake my head not having the will to answer any more questions right now. Travis helps me into his truck and turns the heater on full blast. He closes me in and makes a few phone calls while I wait in deafening silence. All I can hear are the threats from that man. His raspy voice calling me a bitch, threatening to kill me. I don't want to hear what he's saying to the police, and I don't want to be here anymore I just want to go home. But I don't want to be alone. If that robber goes through my glove box he will see where I live and any other information that I have in there. I can't go home, it's not safe, even with all the gadgets that Travis installed. The man could wait outside for me until I came downstairs and then finish me off. I mean he could have done that tonight. He had the gun and everything. A shiver runs down my spine at the thought.

Police cars with their lights on begin piling into the parking lot. Opening the truck door, I take a deep breath and steel myself for all questions to come. Travis comes around to my side and takes my hand.

"You've got this. Just tell them everything you told me then I'll get you out of here." Travis promises in my ear. He wraps his jacket around me as the snow fall begins to pick up around us.

Several police officers come up to me to take my statement. As I recount the events of the evening, a crowd begins to form from people on the streets to the gallery attendees. I clasp my eyes together tightly wishing this was all a dream. I feel like I can't breathe, I've lost the will to keep up this battle. I need to get out of here. To hell with the art showing and the promotion within the company. I want to go somewhere safe and never come back to this place. My soul feels like it was shot tonight, and I don't know if I will ever recover.

"Thank you, Miss McKenzie. If you have any questions just call this number here." The officer tries to hand me the report, making my shaking hands obvious to anyone watching. Travis takes the paper from me and envelopes my hands in his.

"Thank you officers. Please let us know if you find anything." Travis shakes their hands then leads me away.

"You're coming home with me. I want to make sure you are safe." I open my mouth to argue, but it's quickly closed when Travis continues, "Don't argue with me. I will carry you over my shoulder if I have to," he growls.

"It's not that I don't want to I just don't want to be a burden right before Christmas. I'm sure you have other plans that I would interfere with." I whimper as he leads me back to his truck.

"I said don't argue with me, Sarah." He opens his truck and lifts me into the seat buckling me in as well. "I need to make sure you're safe," Is all he says when I give him a quizzical look. The drive to his place is quiet but his hand squeezes mine with a reassuring pressure. As I look out the window, I see the snow storm finally showed up and I have a feeling I will be staying with Travis longer than I planned.

CHAPTER 12

Travis

I can't get the image of a bloodied and frightened Sarah running to me from the darkened parking lot. I had just arrived and was about to step into the gallery when I heard sobs coming from behind me, I turned around just in time to catch her in my arms.

We arrive at my home just in time it seems. The snow fall has doubled since we left the gallery. Sarah has been quiet this whole trip but once we get inside I'm going to fix that. I need to clean her scrapes and get her bandaged up and into some warm clothing.

I pull into the garage and see Harley jumping at the door wagging her tail. Cutting the engine, I look to Sarah who looks like she is still in shock. I slip out of the door and head over to her side.

Opening her door, I break the silence. "You know I will protect you, right? You have nothing to worry about. I'm here." She nods as her head falls into my chest, a soft sob escaping her lips. Pulling her from the truck, I wrap her in my arms and carry her to the door.

"Sit, Harley" I command as I place Sarah down. In the light of my kitchen I can see all the blood coating her delicate skin. Most of it seems to be from when she fell in the parking lot.

"She's beautiful, Travis." Sarah tentatively draws her hand out for Harley to sniff. She doesn't usually warm up to people that often and I'm about to tell Sarah this, but Harley surprises me and goes over to her and stands guard next to her. I think she can sense Sarah's distress.

"Thank you. She's been with me since I retired from the military. She's been a good pup." I mention.

As Sarah enters the living room, she immediately removes her broken heels and sets them aside near the door. It's evident that the moment her feet are liberated from the constricting shoes, she experiences discomfort. With a noticeable limp, she approaches me, wincing in agony with each step. It's apparent that she's in considerable pain, I can't help but feel concerned for her well-being

As I let Harley out, I turn to Sarah with a smile. "Let's get you cleaned up," I say, "and then I'll show you around. Here let me carry you." Sarah nods, seeming grateful for the offer. As we make our way to the bathroom, I can't help but notice how good she feels in my arms.

"You didn't have to carry me but thank you. My feet are killing me." It's the most she's said since she gave her statement to the police. I thought I would need to pull the words from her.

After setting her down on the counter, I ask, "Would you prefer a bath so you can sit and relax?"

"Yes. That would be amazing. Thank you." I start the faucet, stopper the tub, and turn back to her. Her eyes haven't left me since I stepped away. "Travis, thank you for everything. I don't know what I would have done if you hadn't been there. I just keep thinking about what if that man had done it?" She sobs into her hands. "What if he would have shot me or even killed me? Every time I close my eyes, I see him standing before me with that gun." I walk over to her and pull her body flush against my chest. She needs to be grounded to this moment not thinking of what ifs.

"Listen to me, you got away from him. You did exactly what you needed to do to get to safety. No more what ifs. He didn't and you are safe. We might as well be in Fort Knox with the amount of security that I have, alright? There is nothing to be scared of anymore. I'm right here." I kiss the top of her head and see the goosebumps spread over her skin. I affect her just as must as she does me.

The tub is almost full, so I pull back from her. "Now, let's get you in the tub so you can start feeling better and get warm." I pull out a couple towels and set them beside the tub. "If you need any help, I will be right out here." I motion to my bedroom beyond the bathroom. She nods as she slides off the counter and flinches when her feet land on the cool hard tile.

Sarah

The bath felt wonderful, and was exactly what I needed. Travis set out some of his clothes for me and I put them on, rolling the waist of the pants down several times so they wouldn't be too long. I look at myself in the mirror and wince at the spot where the metal barrel cut my forehead. I finger comb my hair and throw the towels into the hamper beside the door. Walking out I find Travis lying on his bed with his phone in hand.

He shoots up as soon as he sees me emerge. "Hey, how are you feeling?"

"Better. Thank you for all this." I gesture to the clothing.

"Stop thanking me for everything, Sarah. I wanted to help, and I wanted you safe. That's why I brought you here. I wasn't going to take no for an answer either." Travis towers over me as he grazes his fingertip along my jawline and down the side of my neck. I close my eyes and whimper at the contact. I want both his hands on me. I want his body pressed against mine. I don't want to think any more about tonight. I want to be right here in this moment with him.

"I need you, kitten. I need to be inside you. I know you want this too," he whispers in the shell of my ear. Goosebumps erupt over my skin at the feel of his hot breath against my neck. He presses me against the wall and uses his feet to spread mine, opening my legs. I know he can feel how hot I am down there. I want this. I *need* this. I want to let go of everything that happened today and let Travis have me. I am acutely aware of my heart beating out of my chest. It's pounding louder than a sledgehammer.

"Yes. Please, Travis. Take me to bed." His large hands grasp my waist pulling me up to his eye level as my legs wrap around him. His hands squeeze my ass as he crashes his lips down on mine. I instantly open up for him and his tongue tangles with mine. Being this close to him I can smell his cologne. It's a mixture of something earthy and sandalwood. He turns us around and heads back toward his bed. He lays me down then slides his body on top of me as he kisses me with such intensity. It's overwhelming.

Dominating.

Passionate.

Controlling.

That's what Travis is.

His lips caress mine so perfectly that I can't help but pull him closer to me. I need him pressed against me. I need to feel the weight of his body against my own. It's a need I feel deep within my core. His hand slides into my hair pulling it tight, he bares my neck to him. Travis slides from my lips, down my neck paying extra attention to the spot behind my ear that makes me go wild. He pulls back for a moment as he takes me in.

"Fuck, you're so sexy in my clothes, but I need to see them off of you." I nod as a whimper escapes my lips. His hands slide down my sides, then he grasps the edge of the shirt and begins trailing it up my body. His eyes never leave mine as he pulls the shirt over my head and tosses it behind him.

He's going so slow I can hardly stand it. "Travis, please!" I whine.

"What do you want, kitten?" he murmurs as he trails hot kisses down my neck, to my collar bone. He doesn't stop there. His hands glide up my waist and stop at my breasts. He takes a nipple in his mouth and nibbles and sucks while stroking the other in his hand. I arch into him. I'm so hot and needy that I can barely stand it.

"I need you." I cry as he chuckles against my skin and looks up at me.

"You have me. What do you really want?" A frustrated sigh leaves my mouth. I've never been asked to say what I wanted but that's exactly what Travis wants me to do. And I bet he won't give it to me unless I say it.

"Please touch me. Everywhere. I need you to relieve the ache I have." It's the best I can do. I need him touch me. I'm hot and wet and need to come like my life depends on it.

"Oh, I think you can do better than that. Tell me, kitten. Where does my girl need me?" Fuck it. I have to say it. I've never talked dirty in my life but here I am about to, it's both exciting and nerve racking.

"Fuck me, Travis. My pussy aches for you. I'm so wet. Please!" I mutter wanting to cover my face. Heat radiates up my body and I feel like he can see the embarrassment written all over me.

"That's my good girl telling me what you want. That wasn't so hard was it?" He slowly descends further down my body nipping and kissing as he goes. He reaches his sweats that I'm wearing and hooks his fingers in them and ever so slowly pulls them down my legs, torturing me more.

"Mmm, what a naughty girl you are not wearing any panties. Maybe you do need that punishment after all." He tosses the pants with the shirt and I am completely naked before him. His eyes turn molten as his gaze zeroes in on my wet pussy. He spreads my legs with his and scoots down the bed until his face is right at my core. "Fuck you smell amazing. I bet you taste even better." He doesn't give me chance to prepare before he lowers his head and licks me from my ass to my clit. My legs begin to shake so he holds them open with his hands. He doesn't come up for air as he licks and sucks, devouring me. Sweat coats my body as my orgasm draws near. I can't hold it off. I'm about to explode when he stops and looks up at me.

"You don't come until I tell you to." Fuck, he looks serious, but I don't know how to hold off.

"But..."

"No buts. You do as I say." He plunges two fingers into my wet depths and I almost come off the bed. His fingers are huge and stretch me more than I've been open before. It makes me wonder what the hell his cock looks like. I couldn't focus on that. All I can focus on is the strength of what was building within me. I could feel it in my belly, I knew that I wouldn't be able to hold off long. His thumb began rubbing circles as he thrust his fingers inside me adding another sensation. Travis was nipping on my inner thigh, and it was almost too much to bear. Almost.

"Come for me, kitten, come on my hand. Let me see you fall apart." It was like he was commanding my body and it obeyed. I shattered before him. It was mind blowing. My body felt like it would perish if he didn't continue his ministrations on me. I came so hard that I nearly blacked out. I was in another realm and the only thing known there was pleasure.

"Yes, yes!" I chanted. The pleasure reached an all-time high and I began drifting back down to Earth. My hips began thrusting in time with his hand wanting more. I needed more. I needed Travis inside me.

"You fell apart beautifully, kitten." He withdraws his fingers from me and licks one clean. "Fuck you taste like heaven. Open." I do as he says, he thrust his fingers into my mouth so I can taste myself. It's tangy and sweet, it's the most erotic thing I've ever done. I think I would be called vanilla, but after this I want to be whatever flavor Travis is.

He pulls his fingers from my mouth with a pop and

pulls his shirt over his head. I'm momentarily stunned at this man's physique. He looks like a fucking Greek god before me.

He smiles at me checking him out. "Like what you see?" I glance up at his face and his brown eyes are hooded with desire. I nod my head unable to speak. I reach up and grab ahold of his pants wanting them off as well. Sitting up, I unhook the belt and pull it free tossing it to the floor. He unbuttons his pants and pulls them down along with his black boxer briefs. I gasp as his large cock springs free. A deep chuckle comes from him. He stands and lets his pants fall to the floor, then he climbs back on the bed and up my body where he settles himself between my legs. I'm growing desperate to feel him inside me, but he doesn't seem to be in any hurry. He is taking this at his pace and I won't convince him otherwise.

He leans down cupping my cheek with one hand while his other arm holds him up. I can feel his cock at my entrance, I wish I could scoot down so it would slip inside me. His eyes bore into mine and I wish I knew what he was thinking.

"Once we do this you will be mine in all ways. There will be no turning back. Your pleasure, your body, your kisses will belong to me. Do you understand? I want you, Sarah, and I intend to keep you." I gasp at his words. I can't believe what he's saying. *How does he know he wants me? How is he so sure?*

"You want me?" I don't mean it to sound insecure but that's the way it comes out.

"I have no doubt in my mind that you belong to me. Say it. Who's are you?" He caresses my cheek then leans in and takes my lips in his. "Don't you feel that? That electricity that sparks between us? I've never felt it before." He slide his tongue between my lips and I moan into his mouth. He's right. His touch is electric on my skin. I felt it the first time he kissed me under the mistletoe. I thought it was just me that felt like that.

"Yes. I feel it." I murmur against his lips.

"Then tell me who you belong to." He demands his eyes boring into mine.

"You, Travis. You have my body." I say as I pull his lips down on mine. I wrap my arms around his neck and kiss him feverishly. It's raw and intense. I grow desperate to have him inside me.

"Soon I will have your heart and soul." He says before he thrust himself to the hilt inside me. I've never felt so full in my life. The pain and the pleasure mix together to form something I've never experienced, but it's the best feeling I've ever had. He pulls himself up to look where we are connected.

"Look at you taking this big cock so well." A shiver runs through me at his praise. I never knew that I was into that but damn, if it doesn't make me hotter. "Does me talking like that turn you on, kitten?" He slams inside me over and over with more force each time. I swear he might be puncturing my cervix with every thrust, but the pain and burn have my hips thrusting up in tandem with his.

"Fuck yes. Don't stop, Travis." I manage to utter. I pull him back down on me, wanting to feel his heavy body pressing me into the mattress. He's so much larger than my small frame, I love being enveloped by him. It makes me feel safe. Safety. That's what I need right now. I feel my mind beginning to wander back to earlier tonight and I don't want to go back there. I close my eyes and will the tears to stay where they are and not fall to my cheeks. That's not what I need to be thinking about right now.

"Keep your mind on me, on us. Stay in the moment, Sarah." Travis commands as I open my eyes to stare up at him. How the hell did he know where my mind was going? He pulls out of me for a moment and I'm about to object when he flips me to my stomach to plunges back inside me. He lifts my ass in the air and spanks it hard. I know leaving a mark in its wake.

"Yes, Sir," I mumble into the pillow.

"That's right, baby girl. Call me Sir." He grabs my ass in his hands and pulls me back against his body as he plunges inside me in a punishing rhythm. I'm overwhelmed with the depth of passion that I am feeling through our connection right now. I can feel him owning my body. It's like his words have materialized between us and I can feel him using me, controlling what I feel. Every move is calculated for maximum pleasure. My orgasm begins to grow, I know it won't be long from this direction.

"I can feel you close again. I want you to come on this cock. I want you to milk all the come out of me. Come for me, kitten." Again, his words trigger a fuse deep inside me. I shoot off like a firecracker, screaming into his pillow, thankful that he doesn't have any close neighbors. I've never been one to be loud during sex, but he is ripping this pleasure out of me, I can't help but to yell out in ecstasy.

"Fuck, take this come. I'm going to fill you up so much that you will feel me dripping out of this perfect cunt for days." His thrusts slow as he dumps jet after jet of come in my hot waiting pussy. His orgasm spurs something inside me and I go off again. By the time I come back down, I am wrung out and exhausted.

"Such a good girl. Who's pussy is this?" He asks as he kisses and nips up my back following the curve to my shoulders

"Yours, Sir. It's yours." I muster out. Without pulling out of me he turns us to our sides and pulls the blankets up over us.

"This is where my cock belongs. I'm going to be inside you every night when we sleep." He pulls me closer and wraps his arm around my middle. I brush the hair out of my face and lean back against him. His short beard scratches my skin as he kisses along my neck continuing up my jaw until he grabs my chin, tilting it toward him. He kisses me with such possessiveness that it gives me chills. He dominates me and I love it. I love being able to let loose and know that I will be taken care of. He is everything I never knew I needed.

I go to sleep without fear in my chest. I know he will protect me. Afterall, he did save me tonight.

CHAPTER 13

4 days til Christmas...

Travis

I wake with my cock throbbing inside Sarah's slick wet pussy. As I pull her body flush against mine, I begin to thrust in and out of her tight hole. She's still full of our joined release making the perfect lubrication. I want to wake her up to an orgasm. She moans in her sleep as she presses her ass against me. I smile because my girl wants my dick first thing in the morning. She just might not be aware that she does.

I love the feel of her soft skin against mine. She's soft where I'm hard, making a perfect piece to fit my puzzle. Brushing the hair from her face, I kiss along her jaw and neck until I hear her gasp.

"Good morning, gorgeous." I kiss along her shoulder and see goosebumps explode over her perfect skin.

"Morning," she whimpers. I can already feel her pussy tightening around me, and I know she's close. I know as soon as she comes that I will too, so I reach around her body and begin circling her clit with my fingers. "Yes! I'm going to come!" She announces.

"Do it, baby. Let me feel you." Every time I tell her to come, her body obeys my orders. I knew she was meant to be mine. Her body already knows who it belongs to. I just need to get her heart on board.

Sarah comes apart spectacularly, taking me with her. I continue to pump into her a few more times until I am completely spent. As a light layer of sweat coats our skin, I kiss along her shoulder and up her neck. Her salty sweet taste is addicting. I pull out of her and immediately miss the wet warmth. I turn her onto her back, so she is looking up at me.

"How about a shower?" I lean down and crash my lips to hers. They are swollen and red from last night, making them more sensitive for her. She moans into my mouth, I swallow it down. I love feeling her beneath me.

"A shower sounds good. I think we are more than dirty enough." She smirks at me and it's that little attitude that I love about her. Well not love. I mean I don't love her, right? It hasn't been long enough, but I can't deny this feeling in my chest when I look at her. When I'm inside her it feels like I am finally home. I can't describe it other than it's utter and complete peace when we're together. Her soul calls out to mine.

I pull her up from the bed and lead her to the bathroom. She tries to cover herself as we walk but I stop her. "Don't you dare hide from me. I've seen every inch of you. There's no need to cover up now." I spank her ass as she walks in front of me leaving the perfect print on there. Claiming her.

She gives out a little yelp and responds, "I'm sorry, Sir, I'm not used to walking around naked with someone watching."

"Damn right you aren't." I catch her elbow and

spin her around to face me. As I pick her up her legs automatically circle around my waist. "I don't want you to be embarrassed or shy around me. I want you to be comfortable. Okay?" She nods and leans up to kiss my lips.

"Did you sleep alright?" I ask when she pulls away as I start the shower.

"I did. I thought I would have bad dreams, but I didn't. I don't remember dreaming anything. I passed right out." Sarah confesses as we get into the shower.

"Good. I was worried you would dream about what happened last night. I stayed up and watched you sleep for a little while until I couldn't keep my eyes open anymore," I admit as the hot water runs down our bodies. Seeing the water run over her slick body has me hard again. It would be so easy to push up inside her with the angle I'm holding her.

"You didn't have to do that. I knew you were there. I think that's what put me at ease," she explains as she leans back into the water getting her face and hair wet. When she leans back up, she bites her lip when she sees the way I'm looking at her.

"I'm going to watch over you and protect you. That's what I'm here for," I tell her. She wraps her arms tightly around me pulling closer to me. I squeeze her ass in my hands, making her moan in my ear. I can feel her hot wet cunt waiting for me. I push her down on my shaft as I push up inside.

Her face morphs into one of pain and I stop thrusting. "Am I hurting you?"

"I'm just a bit sore. I'm okay. It's just been a while for me," she murmurs against my shoulder. "It still feels good, you're just so big."

"Do you want me to stop?" I've slowed my movements but haven't stopped completely. I haven't been able to. Her cunt was made for me and I don't want to leave it.

"No, please don't stop. I need you." It's like magic to my ears.

I hear the slippery sounds every time I drive back inside her and it makes me harder knowing how wet I make her. I lavish her breasts with attention sucking and nipping at both until she is writhing on my dick with her back pressed against the shower wall.

"Don't come until I tell you to." I demand. Her eyes transform into a tumultuous storm. She's so close, she's not going to be able to hold out much longer, but I don't want it to be over. I want to stay cocooned in her slick all day.

"Fuck!" she croons, and I can feel her body tightening, getting ready for its release. "Please, Travis, please let me come."

"You call me Sir when I'm inside you, kitten," I instruct.

"Sorry Sir, please," she pleads with me, begging me with her eyes, growing desperate.

"Come for me baby girl." I demand. Her muscles go taut and she becomes a quivering mess in my hands. I hold her against the wall until she comes down from her orgasm. As I set her down, I hold her in my arms until I know she can stand on her own.

"Let's get cleaned up." She nods and reaches for the shampoo, but I take it from her and squirt some into my palm and start massaging it into her hair.

"You don't have to do that you know. I'm perfectly capable of washing my own hair." There's that sass again.

"You better watch that mouth, kitten. Remember what I told you under the mistletoe." I give her a grin and she playfully punches me in the stomach. "Oh, you've done it now. You've awoken the beast." I tsk as I tickle her. She squeals as I catch her in my arms. A shiver runs through her as she looks me in the eyes. I don't know what it is about this woman, but I need her in my life like I need air to breathe. She crashed into my world, and it's been turned upside down since.

We barely finish showering without having sex again. We can't keep our hands to ourselves. I reach for the heated towels and hand her two, one for her hair. I give her a spare toothbrush then we get dressed for the day. She's back in my clothes that I want to rip off her.

We descend the stairs and Harley is there at the bottom bouncing and waiting to be let out. I open the door and the snow is up to my knees. Fucking hell, I need to call Ryan to make sure everything is alright at the office. Harley jumps over the snow and begins running around the yard, almost falling into the snowy pits. I let her have a little fun before I'm calling her back into the house.

I get Ryan on the phone and he assures me that everything is under control. He lets me know that the office hasn't lost power yet. We go over a few more details before I end the call. Sarah is looking out the window at all the snow still coming down. Walking up behind her, I wrap my arms around her waist and kiss the side of her neck.

"Want some coffee?" I murmur into her ear.

"Of course." She turns slightly in my arms and looks up at me. Leaning down, I capture her lips in mine. She tastes like the mint toothpaste I let her borrow this morning.

"Let me go get some started. How about some pancakes?" I suggest letting her go and head toward the kitchen.

"Wow, you know how to cook pancakes?" she asks, coming over to the kitchen island and taking a seat on one of the stools.

"You'd be surprised at how much I can do." I give her a little wink and she blushes, turning her head so I can't see.

"Well, do you need any help with anything?" she questions.

"Nope. You just sit there and keep me company." I reply as I start up the coffee. I head to the pantry to get the ingredients I need to make pancakes.

Sarah becomes quiet as she turns and continues watching the falling snow.

"Are you doing alright?" I ask coming to stand near her. She doesn't turn and I don't think she heard me. Sarah seems to be in her head thinking about something. I move to stand in front of her and she shakes herself out from her trance. She has unshed tears in her eyes when she looks up at me.

"Sarah, what's going on? What's wrong?" I ask as I stroke her cheek where the tears began to fall.

"I was just thinking." She starts. "About last night. I can't get that man's awful face out of my mind. And the things he said to me just –." She shakes her head and begins wringing her hands together.

"Listen to me. He can't hurt you now. I've got you." I grab her hands as she looks up at me. The sight of her crying guts me and makes me feel murderous. I hate that she's been put in this position. I don't want her to feel scared every time she walks to her car, but I know she will be apprehensive for a while. I can only be here for her and assure her that I won't let anything happen to her while she is with me.

"Thank you, Travis, for everything. You didn't have to bring me here and take care of me, but you did so, thank you." She closes her eyes, and a set of fresh tears roll down her cheeks.

I grasp her chin and pull it up for her to look at me. "What did I tell you about thanking me? I wouldn't be doing this if I didn't want to. I want you here with me, Sarah. Trust me on that. I want you here, baby," I admit. She nods and gives me a small smile. I take that as a win and let go of her so I can finish making her coffee.

Sarah turns back around in her seat to face me, looking better than she did before. Hopefully my talk helped relieve some of her stress. There is no way I would let anything hurt my girl. And she is *my girl*. I told her last night that I wouldn't fuck her unless it meant she was mine and she agreed. I hope she knows she won't be getting rid of me now.

CHAPTER 14

Sarah

"Don't move and don't you fucking scream."

"Look at me, you bitch. No one is coming to save you."

The thoughts of last night keep swirling in my mind and I can't make them stop. One minute I'm fine and the next I'm right back in that parking lot looking at the Devil himself. I need to get my mind under control, I just don't know how. Nothing like this has ever happened to me, I don't want to even leave this house. I'm scared to go outside. I know I'm being irrational, but fear isn't rational.

I try to get my breathing under control as Travis slides me a cup of coffee.

"I don't have all the crazy creamers, but I do have sugar. I hope that's okay. We can try to get to the store today, but I don't know how the roads will be and there's even more snow to come," he says.

"This is fine. I can just add some sugar." I take the mug and spoon in several scoops of sugar and mix it up. It's not the best but it will do. "I don't think we should risk driving in this. We can stay here. Creamer isn't that important," I reply. I don't want to leave the safety of this house.

"That's probably a good idea. I haven't seen what

shape the driveway is in, but if the backyard is anything to go by then I think we would have a situation on our hands. I guess you're stuck here with me for a while." Travis smiles as he begins making the pancakes.

I wonder what I'm going to do about work on Monday. I don't want to even call and see how the gallery show went. I know Madison took over because she knew all the details of the event. I'm thankful that she was there to step up, but I feel dread when I think about work. I know I probably didn't get that promotion even though the events of the evening weren't my fault. Even without the snow, I doubt I would be able to go into the office this week. Well, it would only be Monday and Tuesday because the rest of the week everyone has off for the Christmas holiday.

"What are you thinking so hard about over there?" Travis asks as he flips the pancakes perfectly.

"I was thinking of work. I don't really want to find out how last night went without me there to handle any mishaps." I take another sip of my coffee.

"I'm sure everything went smoothly. You spent months planning it and you had gotten everything ready before you went outside," he mentions as he plates some pancakes then slides them over to me.

"I suppose so. I need to check my phone to see if anyone has tried to get in touch with me. Especially the police." I stand from my chair, but Travis is there to push me back down.

"Breakfast first then we can deal with whatever we have to. Alright?" I nod as he pushes my chair back in. I wait for him to sit down beside me before I dig into the delicious looking breakfast.

"This is so good!" I exclaim with my mouth full of pancakes.

He chuckles as he takes his first bite. "They are pretty good. My mother taught me how to cook before I went to college. So, then I was able to cook for everyone in the Army when I needed to," he states as he dives back in for another bite.

"I didn't get any cooking skills passed down to me. I can cook a mean box meal but that's about it. Even then it's sometimes burned." I blush from embarrassment.

"I'll teach you. We'll have plenty of time since we're snowed in," he replies.

"That sounds fun." We finish eating then clean the kitchen so that there isn't a mess to deal with later. Once everything is finished, we go into the living room and relax on the couch. I look at my phone and see that I have a missed call and voicemail. I listen and it's the police checking in on me and letting me know that they still haven't tracked him down but that they are still working on it. I had it on speaker phone so Travis could hear the news. Once they hang up I look to Travis. His jaw is set and he seems angry.

"Is everything alright?" I ask.

He looks at me with a forced smile. "Yes, I just wish they would find that bastard and throw his ass in jail. I don't want you to be fearful that he hasn't been caught yet."

"Well, thankfully I'm here with you and you have all the security possible." I mention.

"I do. Plus you have me. No one will hurt you as long as you're with me." I let out a sigh of relief and cuddle into him.

Travis turns on the TV while I get a good look at his space. I didn't get a chance to last night, so it's like I'm seeing everything for the first time.

"I can't believe you don't have any Christmas decorations up. I know you are a bit of a grump, but we need to have a tree or something. Please tell me you have some decorations hidden somewhere." I look at him pleadingly. Decorating his house will take my mind off everything. I also don't want to be stuck in a house that doesn't even have some Christmas lights up.

Travis

"I knew you were going to mention that. I was waiting." I sigh and scratch my beard. "I think I do have some decorations we can put up. My mother sent them to me when I bought this house, she knew that I wouldn't buy them myself." I straighten up on the couch as Harley comes over and lays her head in my lap. "I think I put them in a hall closet."

Sarah jumps up clapping her hands together. "Well come on then. Let's go get them. We have a house to decorate." Harley even jumps up and barks at me like she knows what we are talking about. *Traitor.*

"Are you serious? We have to decorate? Can't we just watch a Hallmark movie?" I question even though that sounds equally as painful.

"We can put one on while we decorate. Come on, it will be fun!" she exclaims. I groan as I get up and lead her to the closet that houses the decorations.

She gets excited when she sees all the Christmas stuff

I have. Sarah takes inventory of everything before she looks at me. "You don't have a tree. That's the only thing we're missing." She says downcast.

I can't stand that look on her face, so I cave. "I have some trees in the backyard that would work. Let's get bundled up and go out and look for one." She jumps into my arms and kisses me with so much passion that I find I want to do more things for her to see this reaction.

We get all bundled up. Sarah looks like she is being swallowed up by my clothes but at least she will be warm when we go outside. I get the axe from the garage then open the back door. Harley runs ahead of us creating a trail for us to walk in. I look behind me and see Sarah struggling with the large boots I put on her feet. I laugh out loud at her. The death glare she shoots my way make my balls shrivel up into my body.

I grab her hand and pull her close to me. "How about a piggy back ride? Jump on." She laughs but does as I say. Harley is having the time of her life running and jumping all around us. She loves this time of year. I trudge through the snow to the trees at the end of my property. Once we get there, Sarah jumps down.

"Alright, here we are. Now, your job is to pick the perfect tree," I tell her. She beams up at me then looks around at all the trees she has to pick from.

"Hmm, how about that one?" She points to one in the corner, it has the perfect shape we are looking for.

"We need to make sure the branches are sturdy enough to hold lights and ornaments. Sarah takes a step in that direction and falls flat on her face in a huge pile of snow. She squeals and sits up with her face covered in white powder. I can't help but to laugh.

"Oh, is that funny? How about this?" She gets up and runs toward me then jumps up on me and we both go down laughing the whole way.

She rolls over on her back and we look up at the sky where more snow is falling down on us. It feels like a magical moment. I reach for her hand and take it in mine, squeezing it once then she squeezes back.

"My dad would do that with me when I was younger. He would squeeze my hand once and it meant 'I love you'. It was our thing until he passed away," Sarah mentions as she continues to look up at the falling snow.

"I'm sorry. I didn't mean to bring that memory back for you." I begin to let her hand go but she holds on tighter.

"No. I liked it. I like remembering the good times with him." She looks over at me and smiles. I grasp her hand tighter not wanting to let go. "I think we need to cut down this tree and get back inside before we get snowed over," she jokes.

"I agree." I stand and then pull her up, our hands staying connected. "Are we sure this is the one?" I ask before I begin chopping it down.

"Yes, it's perfect. Do you have a stand to put it in? I didn't even think to ask you before."

"Actually, I do. It's in the garage. I suppose it was waiting for this Christmas to make itself useful." I pick up the axe that I dropped and let go of Sarah's hand so I can cut down the tree she chose. My hand feels bare without hers in it.

It doesn't take long for me to cut it down, then we get

back in the house. We shake it as much as we can to get the extra snow off before we bring it in with towels. As I attach the base, Sarah begins bringing down the decorations from the hallway. I situate the tree off to the side of the fireplace, right in front of the windows to the back porch.

"Oh, it's perfect Travis!" Sarah smiles the brightest of smiles at me.

"I'm glad. Now, it's time to decorate it. What do we do first?" I ask.

"Lights always go first." She digs through the bins and pulls out several boxes of white Christmas lights. "These are perfect." She hands me a box and we both take them out and begin unraveling them. Sarah takes her strand behind the tree then plugs them in. "So, we start at the bottom and go to the top." She goes around the tree back and forth until she can no longer reach. Then I take over for her and emulate the way she was putting them into the tree. She stands back squinting her eyes.

"What are you doing?" I ask.

"This is how you tell if you missed any big spots. You just concentrate on looking at the lights and it shows you bare places. I think we got it right the first time. You aren't so bad at this." She holds her hand up for me to slap.

"I didn't say I was bad at it. I just never took the time to decorate." I return her high-five.

"Alright then, well, grab some ornaments and start putting them on there while I make some bows with this ribbon. Make sure you space them out." She smirks at me.

After a couple hours, the Christmas tree is done and Sarah and I are on the couch enjoying the view. "I have to admit my place was missing some holiday cheer. Thank you, Sarah, for bringing it here." I take her hand in mine and bring it to my lips pressing small kisses to her fingers.

"Thank you for chopping down one of your trees for me. It may not be a real Christmas tree but it's my favorite that I've ever decorated." We snuggle in closer as we take in the decorations. It's getting darker outside and I hear Sarah's stomach rumble. I guess we worked through lunch.

"What would you like for dinner? I told you I would teach you how to cook." I remind her.

"Something easy. How about pasta?" she asks.

"Sure, come on. Pasta it is." We make our way to the kitchen and spend the next hour making the most delicious Alfredo. We are a great team and I can't help but to be in awe of this beautiful creature that fell into my lap. Literally.

CHAPTER 15

3 days til Christmas...

Sarah

I wake to Travis sliding in and out of me slowly, his hot breath coating my skin. I could get used to waking up like this every morning. My breathing picks up and my heart accelerates as he picks up his pace.

"I know you're awake, kitten. Open those gorgeous eyes for me. I want to see you as I fuck you into this mattress." I gasp at his words and open my eyes. He slips out of me and pushes me on my back and thrusts back inside. "That's better. I want to see those sexy green eyes of yours." He kisses across my chest and up the side of my neck until he whispers, "You're so wet for me, baby." I gush at his words. "I love sleeping inside of you because I get to do this first thing in the morning." Travis pushes the hair from my face and leans down capturing my lips with his. I pull him closer as I wrap my arms around his neck. I can't get enough of him. He's addicting. The pull between us is magnetic and I don't want to fight it.

Fuck, he feels so good. I've never had sex this explosive or passionate. Travis takes it to a whole new level. One that I'm sure no other man could come close to. I push my hips up to meet his slow thrusts because I need more. More of him, more of everything.

"Someone is being greedy this morning," he murmurs against the shell of my ear.

"I just – need more. Harder, Sir." That spurs him on. He picks up my legs and throws them over his shoulders. He's deeper than he's ever been. The pain and pleasure mix to make this extraordinary feeling begin to rise in my belly.

"How's that? Is that hard enough for you, kitten?" he asks with a devilish grin. "I've got something for you since you love Christmas so much. I thought you wouldn't mind getting tied up with some ribbon." He pulls out some purple satin ribbon and ties my hands together and then pushes them over my head. "Keep those there," he commands.

"Yes, Sir," I stammer as he pounds harder into me. Travis continues to hit the perfect spot inside me and my body draws tight. "I'm going to come!" I yell closing my eyes. Wave after wave of pleasure courses through me.

"I didn't tell you to come yet, did I?" Travis pulls out of me so quickly and flips me on my stomach drawing my ass into the air. He slams back inside me then gives me the hardest spanking of my life. My breath leaves me for a moment before he spanks the other side of my ass. He uses his hands to smooth over the pain but it still tingles. This isn't how I imagined I'd wake up this morning. My hands are still bound but I squeeze the sheets to ground myself to this moment.

"That's what happens to naughty girls that don't listen. Are you going to listen to me now? Who tells you when to come?" he asks.

"Yes, I'll listen. I'm sorry, Sir. You tell me when to come," I cry into the pillow.

"That's my good girl. Now, you're going to come for me again," he growls from behind me. He reaches around and begins rubbing my clit faster and faster until I'm a quivering mess. I don't know how much longer I can hold out but I don't dare do anything yet.

"I can feel you clenching around me. I know you're close. Do you want to come?" he whispers into my ear.

"Yes! Please, Sir!" I murmur as he continues to dominate me in every way.

"Good girl. Come for me. Come on my cock. I want to feel you pulsing around me, baby."

"Ah, oh yes," I sob as my orgasm ricochets through my body touching all my nerve endings in its path. My eyes roll back as the pleasure wracks my body. Travis knows how to use my body like a damn instrument and he's the master.

"Fuck, you take me so well. Do you feel that? Do you feel this big cock filling you up?" He continues to pound into me slowing his pace little by little. "Your cunt wants to swallow me up, kitten. Fuck, you feel so good wrapped so tightly around me." Travis pulls out slowly as I cry out. He turns me back over. And slides ever so slowly back inside me. He's still hard somehow but I'm not complaining. Heat pulses through my blood from where we are connected. He slides his hands up my sides stopping at my breasts. "I didn't get to give these any attention earlier," he says with a smirk as he descends, sucking my nipple into his mouth. His hand grasps the other and tweaks it in the same rhythm as his tongue and teeth. It's not long before I'm writhing under his sweat glistened body as he lavishes my breasts with attention.

"Oh, Travis you feel so good. Everything you do feels

so good." I moan.

"It feels that good because you're mine. Mine alone now and forever. Your body knows who possesses it, kitten." He looks me in the eyes and I can see the seriousness of what he is saying.

I draw in a breath with a faint "oh" as he presses even deeper inside me.

"I know you feel it too. It isn't just me. I've never felt anything more electric in my life," he admits. Travis traces my jaw with his fingers, then runs them along my neck giving me chills.

"I can feel it," I confess. He continues to slide in and out of me at an agonizingly slow pace, it feels like we have crossed over into something deeper than fucking. Dare I say making love? It's real and wild but I feel like our souls are involved now. I can feel his soul colliding with mine.

Travis cups my face in his hand, his thumb caressing my lips as he stares into my eyes. Then he slowly presses his lips to mine. It's slow and sweet and says everything he isn't. He's claiming me.

"Come for me, kitten. Shatter for me and only me." His words command my body. He sets off an orgasm within me that had been slowly building and finally reached it's peak. My body quivers under his as I feel his muscles go taut. His release barrels through him and the electricity between us grows to an all-time high. I can feel his cock pulse inside me while he doesn't release my lips. His thrusts stop as he looks up at me. He lays down beside me and pulls me along with him. Resting my head on his chest, he kisses my forehead and somewhere along the way I fall back asleep.

◆ ◆ ◆

Travis

Harley jumps on the bed letting me know she needs to go out. Sarah stirs next to me but doesn't wake up. I think I wore her out this morning. I slip out of bed, trying not to wake her. Pulling on a pair of sweats I follow Harley down the stairs and out the door into the snow. It looks like a few more inches fell last night. I shut the door and head to the kitchen to put on a pot of coffee. Just as I pour the water in, the electricity goes out. It's a good thing I have a generator.

I head out to the garage and am getting it set up when Sarah appears at the door with Harley by her side. Those two have grown quite fond of each other the past couple days.

"I heard Harley scratching at the door to be let in. I think she was cold out there this morning," Sarah says as she wraps the blanket from the couch around her shoulders.

"Sorry she woke you. I was going to let you sleep in a bit more," I reply as I crank up the generator. After making sure everything is set correctly, I walk back into the house. Leaning down I give Sarah a quick kiss and head back to the kitchen to finish the coffee.

Harley paws at her bowls making me chuckle. "I haven't forgotten you, you spoiled pup." I fill her bowls then watch Sarah go behind the Christmas tree to plug it in.

"I called my boss this morning and told her what was going on and not to expect me this week. She was fine with it, especially with everything that happened Saturday. She wants to have a meeting with me when we all get back to the office," she states as she walks into the kitchen and sits. "I think it might be about the promotion."

"That's great. I know you were worried about what she was going to say." I pour two cups of coffee and hand one over to Sarah along with the sugar.

"Thank you. Coffee is definitely needed today," she says with a wink. I know exactly what she means. I need this extra fuel as well.

My phone begins to ring in my pocket. Taking it out I see that it's Ryan calling, probably to tell me about the power situation. I answer it, putting it on speakerphone so I can get some breakfast going.

"What's up, Ryan?" I ask.

"Tank, the power went out but I have the generators up and running. All the equipment seems to be online except for a few. I called the power company to see which areas and clients don't have power. Other than that, everything is fine." I pull out some bacon and eggs as Ryan finishes his spiel.

"Good work. There's nothing we can do for those people until their power comes back so just hang tight," I answer as I pick the phone up.

"You doing okay, boss?" Ryan asks.

"Yep, just had to crank up my generator so I figured you would be calling soon. Have you checked the weather recently? Is the snowstorm almost over?"

"It's supposed to clear out by this evening, but the temperatures are still dropping so it may turn into ice. Everyone is being told to stay indoors unless absolutely necessary," he states.

"Thanks for the info." I pause for a moment thinking back to something Sarah mentioned to me the night she got attacked. "Hey Crash, can you do me a favor?"

"Anything, Tank. What's up?" he asks.

"How are the roads up your way and in the city?"

"They are clear. The trucks keep coming through to clear the snow."

"I need you to get the guys to help you on this one. When Sarah's car was stolen, he took her donations for the Toys For Tots charity. I need you to go to the toy store at the Galleria and stock up on toys for those children. Get as much as you can fit into your truck and use the company credit card."

"Will do, boss."

"Thanks, man." Ryan hangs up as I slide my phone back into my pocket.

"Travis, that's too much. I can't ask you to do that for me." she says with a frown.

"I told you that I would take care of it. This is me taking care of it. You don't want them to go without do you? Those toys in your trunk are probably long gone by now." I walk in front of her and take her hands in mine. "Let me do this for you."

"I'll pay you back for everything." She rushes out.

"No, you won't. I am doing this for your peace of mind and for those children. I don't need repayment."

"Thank you, Travis. You don't know how much this means to me." she gushes then she get serious for a moment. "Did he just call you Tank?" Sarah asks with a smile on her face.

"He did. That was the name I was given in the Army. Is that funny to you?" I ask with a quirk of my brow.

"No, not at all. It's cute. I like it," she admits with a laugh.

"Cute? You think my nickname is cute?" I move around the counter to stand in front of her.

"Yes, very cute. Do I get to call you Tank as well?" she questions with a smirk on her lips.

I pick her up, throwing her over my shoulder as she squeals and kicks her legs. "No, you may not. You can call me, Sir." I pop her ass then toss her on the couch. She shrieks as she bounces up a couple times. I jump on the couch caging her in, she giggles and surrenders herself to me.

"I'm sorry," she laughs, "I'm sorry, *Sir!*" she enunciates but it's too late. My hands go to her sides and dig in tickling her until she can't take it anymore.

Harley comes over and jumps up on the couch trying to paw me away from Sarah. "I'm not hurting her, am I, kitten?"

"No," she says between fits of laughter. "Get him Harley! Us girls have to stick together," she chuckles. "Okay, okay! Mercy!" she shouts. I laugh right along with her. She has the most perfect laugh. Well not just the laugh, everything is perfect about her. I stop the assault on her ribs then lean over bringing my mouth to hers. As I pull away from her lips, I plant kisses on her cheek, forehead, and tip of her nose.

"Come on, let's go make some breakfast." As I sit up,

I grab her hand bringing her along with me We head to the kitchen and get started on breakfast. Sarah cranks up some Christmas music on her phone and we dance around the kitchen making eggs and bacon.

The rest of the day goes by quietly as we snuggle on the couch watching TV and talking. More snow continues to fall as we light the fireplace and burrow in closer to watch another Christmas movie.

CHAPTER 16

1 day til Christmas...

Travis

The snow finally stopped falling and the plows were out clearing out the roads leading to the city. We are no longer snowed in, which means Sarah gets to go home. There's an ache in my chest at the thought of her leaving me here. Harley would miss her for sure but more than that, I would miss her. She brought life to this house and made it a home.

Sarah comes down the stairs fresh from a shower with damp hair. I can smell my soap on her, I want to shout it from the rooftops that she is mine. That I have claimed her.

"Good morning, kitten. Coffee?" I ask as I pour her a cup.

"Of course. I can't start the day without it." I slide the mug over to her along with the sugar.

"The roads have been cleared and the snow seems to have finally stopped." I mention as I take a sip of my coffee, which suddenly tasting bitter on my tongue.

"Oh, wow. That was fast." She looks up at me with a face I can't decipher. "I guess you want to get me out of your hair. I guess you can take me home whenever you want." She says quickly not making eye contact with me but staring into her coffee.

"I didn't mention it because of that. I thought you would be ready to get back to your apartment." I watch her closely trying to understand what she is feeling.

"I, um, I'm actually a little scared to go back to my apartment since the incident. That man has all my information in the glove box. He could be waiting at my apartment to finish me off since I know what he looks like. I'm scared, Travis." Sarah begins to hyperventilate and I rush over to her.

"Breathe, Sarah. You have to breathe. In through your nose and out through your mouth. Do what I'm doing. In and out, baby." She begins to breathe regularly after a bit of coaxing. "Good girl. Now, listen to me. There is nothing wrong with you wanting to stay here. We could go get you some clothes and then come back or we can just stay here a bit longer. Whatever you are comfortable with." I run my fingers down the side of her cheek, wiping her tears away. "I'm here to take care of you. Whatever you need."

"Th-thank you. I don't know what I would I do without you, Travis."

"Thankfully you don't have to find out." I kiss her softly.

We spent the day playing games and watching terribly cheesy Christmas movies but it was one of the best days of my life. It was simple and easy. Everything with Sarah is easy. It's like we were made for each other. We fit together like perfect puzzle pieces. She belongs with me, by my side. I can't help thinking this is how it's supposed to be.

"I win again, old man," she says with a smirk.

"Old man, huh? I don't remember you complaining this morning," I tsk from my seat on the ground. We laid out some blankets in front of the roaring fire that I've been wanting a reason for her to join me on for a while. Now seems like the perfect invitation.

"Get your ass over here, kitten. Crawl on your hands and knees. I want that ass up in the air." I give her a look that dares to be argued with.

"Yes, Sir." She moves off the couch and gets on her hands and knees.

"Keep those eyes on me. Now, come." I can see the fire in her eyes. She wants to disobey me. She likes the punishments a little too much. She starts crawling toward me as her ass sways in the air. There is an insatiable lust between us. I can't get enough of her perfect pussy clamping down on me.

"Now, strip and lay down. I want to see my pussy." She's got those lips that makes me want to fuck her in the mouth but there is time for that later. I want my cock inside her sweet juicy cunt. She was built to please me. She bites down on her lips as she lays before me naked and waiting.

"You're a good girl but you want to be naughty don't you, baby?" she nods looking to the fire then back at me. I can see her thoughts in her eyes. She wants me just as badly.

"I need you," Sarah whines as she slides her body back and forth on the blankets. Pulling the shirt over my head, I lean over her body kissing up the inside of her legs, missing the spot she needs me the most. I continue up her body, nipping then soothing the sting away with my tongue. She gasps as I make my way higher. She runs her hands through my hair and tries to pull me closer, but she can't dictate where I'm going.

"Where do you need me? Where does my naughty kitten want my tongue?" I ask as I bite down gently on her nipples before sucking them into my mouth. I want to lick and savor every fucking inch of her creamy skin. My need for her is like a raging inferno. It gets stronger and stronger the closer I am to her.

She looks away as she nibbles on her bottom lip, then looks back at me with an intensity that tells me she knows exactly what she wants.

"My pussy needs you. I want you inside me. Please, Sir." I chuckle at her innocence. She isn't used to asking for what she wants, but soon she will be. I lean up and pull my sweats from my body and crawl back up her body.

"Does this cock look like an old man's to you? Have I not shown you how I use it properly? Maybe you need a little reminder of how I can wreck that little pussy of yours." She whimpers at my words. "Do I need to show you, kitten?" She nods with a wicked smile on her face.

"Please, Daddy, fuck me." My cock jumps at the name. Fuck, I want to slam into her.

"I am your Daddy, aren't I? You need someone to take care of you?" She nods shyly, still nibbling on her lip. I drag my hand down her body until I get to her wet pussy.

"Does Daddy make you this wet? Tell me who owns this little pussy and I'll give you what you want." I circle her clit with my thumb as I push two finger into her. "Ever since the day that I got a taste of this sweet pussy it's been mine. You are mine. Say it," I demand.

"I'm yours, only yours." I line my cock up to her entrance and thrust inside in one motion.

"Fuck, you were made for me, baby." A scream erupts from her mouth. I take her chin in my hand, bringing her lips to meet mine. We both grow desperate as we ravage each other. Sarah pulls my face closer to hers and begins to thrust her hips up and down my shaft.

Her nails dig into my shoulders, I'm sure leaving marks. I slap her ass hard. An audible gasp slips from her sweet little mouth. I know she likes some pain, that's why she practically begs to be punished. She rocks in tandem with my thrusts and soon she is at her peak. I feel her walls clamp down on me.

"Come for me, kitten. Come for Daddy." I keep thrusting in harder and harder with every motion. I start to feel the tingle at the base of my spine, I know I won't last much longer. I start rubbing her clit in rough circles, causing her to jolt in my arms.

"Yes! Fuck! Yes, Daddy! I'm coming!" My orgasm quakes through me like electricity and jet after jet of my come dumps into Sarah's tight little pussy. I begin to slow my strokes as she starts to go limp in my arms from exhaustion.

I crash my lips down on her ravaging her mouth like I just did to her cunt. I need to claim her everywhere. She threads her fingers through my hair and the sensation sends shocks through my system. I love this girl. I fucking love Sarah.

I reluctantly pull out of her and pull her into my arms in front of the fire. "You are amazing, you know that?" I ask.

"I think you are pretty great too." She yawns and falls

asleep in my arms. I cradle her closer to me and eventually pull her up from the floor and carry her to our bed. Yes, it's our bed. I don't want her to go back to her apartment unless it's to get her things. I fall asleep to thoughts of her living here and raising a family together.

Daddy. I could be one.

CHAPTER 17

Christmas Day

Sarah

I wake to the sound of Christmas carols playing downstairs. I roll over feeling the spot where Travis was, it's cool to the touch. He must have wanted me to sleep in. I walk to the en suite and jump in the shower. The hot water feels good compared to the temperature Travis keeps his home. It's like I'm staying in a frozen tundra. I smile to myself when I think of him. It's been a whirlwind couple weeks with this past week being here with Travis has been magical. I never imagined I'd ever really be snowed in. I thought it was just a silly trope that I see only on the Hallmark channel but here we are.

I wrap myself in a towel and head into Travis' closet to find more clothes to wear. That's been the worst thing, not having my own clothes or toiletries. I pick out some more sweatpants and a Princeton sweatshirt. As I'm pulling them over my head, I hear Travis coming up the stairs.

"I thought you would still be sleeping." He wraps his arms around me and lifts me up to his chest. My feet automatically wrap around his waist. "I was going to wake you up in a manner that's been proved most effective in the past."

"Oh, is that so? I would have stayed in bed then, had I known. Too bad I already had a shower," I say with a smirk.

"Yes, too bad indeed. Well, come downstairs. I have a surprise for you." Travis puts me down and leads me to the kitchen where a breakfast feast awaits us.

"I can't believe you did all this for me," I mention as I look around at everything. There's pancakes, fruit, bacon, eggs, and even cinnamon rolls. "How long have you been up? This must have taken forever! We could feed an Army!" I exclaim.

"Well, that's not too far off." I look at him with a puzzled look. "I invited the guys over for a Christmas breakfast. It will give everyone a chance to meet you. I hope that's okay?" Travis asks with genuine concern in his eyes.

"Sure, the more the merrier! Although, I'm not really dressed for the occasion." I look down at myself and wonder if there is anything I can do to make this makeshift outfit better. Doubtful, unless I get the scissors out and start cutting. Oh well, this is as good as its going to get.

Travis comes up behind me and squeezes my waist. "They will love you, stop worrying." A knock sounds at the door and Harley jumps up from her bed, running to greet the first person to arrive. Travis walks to the door and welcomes several men into his home. They all slap each other on the backs as they lean in to give man hugs.

I hear the pounding of my heart in my ears, I'm suddenly extremely nervous. Not at meeting new people but at meeting his team. This makes everything between us become real. Our little bubble is popping and I'm not sure I'm ready for it.

Travis pulls me from my thoughts. "Sarah, I want

you to meet the guys. This is Ryan "Crash" Stevenson, Jack "Ghost" Ryder, Damien "Jester" Holloway, Colby "Mack" Thompson, and Sonny "Demo" Campbell. Guys, this is Sarah McKenzie, my girlfriend." He comes over and wraps his arm around me.

"Nice to meet you all. I don't know if I'll remember your names so you might have to remind me at some point." Each member of the team comes up to me and shakes my hand and reminds me of their names. Damien is the last to come up to me and gives me a hug and says, "Thank you for getting him into the Christmas spirit. We've never seen him this happy, nor have we ever seen a damn Christmas tree in this house." He smiles at me and joins the rest of the crew in the kitchen.

We gather around the feast and Travis decides to say a few words. "Thank you all for coming. I didn't want to spend another holiday without my men by my side along with a very special Sarah who brought out the Christmas cheer in me. So, everyone grab a plate and dig in. We have plenty!" Travis comes over to me and kisses the top of my head. I hear someone in the background say "aww", but I'm solely focused on the man in front of me.

"Want me to make you a plate, baby?" he asks with a smile that could light the darkest of days.

"That would be great. Thank you, *Sir*." I whisper to see his reaction. His nostrils flare and his eyes darken with lust. I bite my bottom lip as he adjusts his pants, turning away from me and grabbing a plate.

Once every ounce of food is eaten and all the bellies are full, the men say their goodbyes and leave us alone. Harley goes back to her bed and snuggles in as Travis leads me to the couch. I plop down and stare up at him waiting for him to take a seat.

"I have something for you. I was waiting until everyone left to give it to you." He goes to the Christmas tree and pulls out a wrapped box that I hadn't even noticed was there. He leans down on his knees in front of me as he places the box in my hands.

"How-when did you do this? I don't have anything for you, Travis." I turn the box in my hands slowly. It's beautifully wrapped in blues and silvers. It would match my Christmas tree at home and I wonder if he did that on purpose.

"I got it before the incident on Saturday. I've had it the whole time you've been here but I wanted to wait until today to give it to you." He looks up at me and pushes the hair out of my face. "Open it, kitten." He pulls away and sits on his knees waiting for me to open the present.

Slowly I remove the ribbon. I don't know why I'm so nervous all of a sudden. I guess its just from the unknown. I take the top off the box and instantly my breath catches in my chest. Tears begin forming in my eyes and I set the box down on my knees and pull out the snow globe that Travis and I saw at the Galleria. He remembered. The snow globe is almost identical to the one I used to have all those years ago. There is a man holding his daughter's hand and looking up at the Eiffel Tower. I can't hold back the tears any longer.

"You remembered. You remembered this snow globe." I cry as I shake it and the snow twirls around.

"Of course I remembered. I could tell it meant a lot to you, so I went back the next day and purchased it for you."

I set the snow globe aside and jump into Travis' waiting arms. "Thank you so much. You don't know what this means to me!" I sob as I kiss him with all the love in my heart.

Travis pulls back and cups my cheeks. "I love you, Sarah. I have for a while now, but I just didn't know how to tell you. I adore you and I never want to be without you."

"I love you, too." I murmur against his lips before his slam down on mine. He kisses me like he will never let me go, I don't want him to.

I'm in love with him. I don't know when it happened and I can't explain it. I think my heart recognized a kindred soul in his. I don't think love has a timeline, it's wild and unpredictable. And in two weeks I fell for a man I barely knew. I don't think it matters if its weeks, months or even years, when you know you know. I love Travis James. He saw me at my most vulnerable time when I was mugged but I felt completely safe in his arms. He's so deeply tied to every feeling I've ever had of love. That's how I know I love him.

"Merry Christmas, Sarah." He takes my hand in his and squeezes it twice. My heart flutters.

"Merry Christmas, Travis." I squeeze his in return.

Life isn't always a holiday, it's not always Christmas trees and singing carols. It has conflict and problems but at the end of the day what matters most is if you smiled through the pain. If you fought for what you wanted and didn't get steamrolled by life.

ABOUT THE AUTHOR

L. B. Martin

L.B. Martin lives in South Carolina with her husband and two children. She spends her free time reading, writing, and drinking all the coffee. L.B. majored in English literature in college with a minor in British Lit. Her husband is a gaming streamer, so when he is playing, she is reading away. She grew up reading the Harry Potter series and became obsessed with the written word.  When she's not reading and writing, L. B. loves to express herself through tattoos and piercings. She is surrounded with music to cleanse and rejuvenate her spirit. Writing began as a form of therapy.

L.B. Martin began writing as a form of therapy.

"My words spill from my mind to the pages in effort to rid myself of the demons tucked away inside. My hope is that readers will be immersed into my world and come out feeling hopeful and full of purpose." -L.B. Martin

BOOKS IN THIS SERIES

Knight Publishing Series

Knight Publishing Company, the largest publishing company in the U.S., is not only known for its best-selling books but also for the men who own the company. Miles and Sebastian Knight are two of the most eligible bachelors in New York. These two brothers are known for their playboy life styles but no one seems to be able to tame them until fate blows their way. Will these two ever meet their match? And is there a third Knight that no one knows about? Pick up this series and find out!

The Write Knight

Life isn't always a fairytale...

Lizzie hasn't had the easiest life. With old wounds from childhood trauma and boyfriends past weighing her down, she has sworn off all men, even if she does meet one that checks all her boxes. He will just break her heart, right? They all do in the end. Maybe Miles Knight is just what Lizzie needs to conquer her inner demons.

Miles is used to being in the spotlight but when a chance encounter with a mysterious Lizzie, who doesn't know who he is, takes place, he knows without doubt that he has to see her again. Will he be able to find her? And when he does, will he be enough to override the trauma that she has experienced.

The Silent Knight

Life isn't always a holiday...

Sarah's quite content making her own way in life when she literally crashes into the story book version of a tall, handsome, stranger. Finding a man was not on her very tight agenda, but she isn't immune to his charms, or his dirty mouth.

Former military Master Sergent, Travis James, loves a challenge. When a cute, mouthy blonde falls on him in the hallway, he can't help but think, challenge accepted. He turns on the charm and becomes her knight in shining armor, but will she put him straight into the friendzone?

Unforeseen circumstances have Travis playing the hero once again, landing them snowed in together for Christmas, with only one bed.

Will Sarah let him take control and keep her safe, or will her mouth get her in trouble once again?

The Starry Knight

Life isn't always a work of art...

Stormy was on a path of destruction until she ran into a power greater than her own. An arrogant bosshole with a penchant for driving her mad. But she had a secret that she was trying to escape and needed a place to work. She had a fire inside her she refused to allow any man to snuff out—or so she thought.

Sebastian was the most eligible playboy bachelor in New York City until a tempest crashed into his life overturning everything in her wake. She was chaos, a hurricane, a force to be reckoned with, and he wanted nothing to do with her... until he did. Suddenly, he felt something ignite inside him that he never knew possible. So, he decided to keep her—whether she liked it or not.

Secrets never stay hidden though and soon they must overcome a whirlwind of obstacles to refrain from scrapping the canvas and starting over.

This is an office, enemies to lover's romance with a steamy, happily ever after.

The Last Knight

Life isn't always a battle...

Samuel's and Marcy's story will release May 17, 2024.

TO LEARN MORE ABOUT L. B. MARTIN
linktree

Made in the USA
Middletown, DE
30 December 2023